You let the tomb robbers pass by the alcove. They are discussing how they killed the owner of the magical rope somewhere ahead in the underworld.

Their voices recede into the distance and you are just about to step back into the corridor when you feel a bandage-swathed arm clamp on to your shoulder. You swing round to find yourself confronted by a bandage-clad mummy staring at you through a slit in the cloth wound round its head. It holds a wickedly curved dagger in one of its hands. You must fight.

Gamebooks from Fabled Lands Publishing

by Jamie Thomson and Dave Morris:

Fabled Lands 1: The War-Torn Kingdom
Fabled Lands 2: Cities of Gold and Glory
Fabled Lands 3: Over the Blood-Dark Sea
Fabled Lands 4: The Plains of Howling Darkness
Fabled Lands 5: The Court of Hidden Faces
Fabled Lands 6: Lords of the Rising Sun

by Dave Morris:

Castle of Lost Souls

In preparation:

by Dave Morris:

Heart of Ice
Down Among the Dead Men
Necklace of Skulls
Once Upon a Time in Arabia

by Jamie Thomson and Mark Smith:

Way of the Tiger 1: Avenger
Way of the Tiger 2: Assassin
Way of the Tiger 3: Usurper
Way of the Tiger 4: Overlord
Way of the Tiger 5: Warbringer
Way of the Tiger 6: Inferno

Curse of the
Pharaoh

Oliver Johnson

First published 1985 by Grafton Books

This edition published 2013 by Fabled Lands Publishing,
an imprint of Fabled Lands LLP

www.sparkfurnace.com

ISBN-13: 978-1490996394
ISBN-10: 1490996397

HOW TO USE THIS BOOK

You are a skilled adventurer who has roamed over much of the known world. In your yearning for constant challenge and the excitement of battle you have fought trolls, ores, goblins, mad warlocks and many other strange and terrifying opponents.

And you have always won. The years of adventure have honed your reflexes and fighting skills so that few could hope to stand against you in single combat.

To determine just how good an adventurer you are, you must use the dice:

- Roll two dice. Add 20 to this number and enter the total in the VIGOUR box on your Character Sheet. This score represents your strength, fitness and general will to survive. Any wounds you take during your quest are subtracted from your VIGOUR score - if it ever reaches zero you are dead.

- Roll one die. Add 3 to the number rolled and enter the total-in the PSI box on your Character Sheet. The higher this score, the better you are at resisting spells cast at you and the more sensitive you are to psychic impressions.

- Roll one die, add 3 and enter the total in the AGILITY box. This score reflects how nimble you are. You will need a high AGILITY to scale walls, leap across chasms, and so on.

YOUR NAME

Personalize your adventure persona by thinking of a heroic name. You might call yourself Lucas Starkiller or Sir Bergan the Bold, Lady Angela Centuri or Li Chun the Black Dragon, or any other name you can think of. Imagine what sort of adventurer you are first - a noble

CHARACTER SHEET

VIGOUR	Current score:	TREASURE
		30 gold pieces
AGILITY	Current score:	
PSI	Current score:	

ITEMS

sword
one half of a stone tablet

OPPONENTS

VIGOUR	*VIGOUR*
VIGOUR	*VIGOUR*
VIGOUR	*VIGOUR*

knight, a crafty rogue, a dashing swordsman or a rugged Viking, perhaps - and then choose a name to reflect that.

VIGOUR, AGILITY and PSI

Your VIGOUR will change constantly during the adventure - every time you are wounded, in fact. You may acquire healing potions or find refreshment on your journey. This may restore some of the VIGOUR points you have lost owing to wounds - but unless you are told otherwise your VIGOUR will never exceed its original value. This is your *normal* VIGOUR score, and you must keep a careful note of it.

Your AGILITY and PSI are less likely to change, although this is possible. Spraining your ankle, for example, might reduce your AGILITY by 1 point. A magic helmet might increase your PSI. But, as with VIGOUR, your AGILITY and PSI will never exceed their *normal* scores unless you are specifically told otherwise.

COMBAT

During the course of your adventure, you will often come across a monster or human enemy whom you must fight. When this happens, you will be presented with an entry something like this:

107

The Giant tears a branch from a nearby tree and lumbers towards you. There is nowhere to run - you must fight.

GIANT   VIGOUR 15

Roll two dice:
score 2 to 6   You are hit; lose 3 VIGOUR points
score 7 to 12   The giant loses 3 VIGOUR points

If you win, turn to **273**.

At the start of every combat, you should record your opponent's VIGOUR score in an empty Encounter Box. You then roll the dice to see who has been wounded. If both you and your opponent still have VIGOUR scores of more than 0, you must continue to roll the dice until the VIGOUR score of either you or your enemy is reduced to 0 - indicating death. Keep note of the VIGOUR scores on your Character Sheet and in the Encounter Box.

ESCAPING FROM COMBAT

In some cases you may be engaged in combat and find yourself losing. If given the option, you may FLEE from the combat. Your enemy will, however, attempt to strike a blow at your unguarded back as you turn to run. To represent this, whenever you choose to FLEE you should roll two dice and compare the total to your AGILITY score. If the dice roll *exceeds* your AGILITY then you have been hit (losing 3 VIGOUR points) as you FLEE. If the dice roll is *less than or equal to* your AGILITY score, however, you dodge your opponent's parting blow and escape without further injury.

ITEMS

You are certain to come across a number of ITEMS on your travels. Some of these may turn out to be useless - or even harmful - but sometimes even the most insignificant-looking acquisition can prove vital to your quest. You should fill in items on your Character Sheet as you acquire them and cross them off as they are discarded or used up.

Leaving aside such obvious possessions as your clothing, backpack, etc, which need not be listed, you begin with several important items. These have already been filled in on your Character Sheet:

- your sword
- half a stone tablet
- 30 gold pieces

YOUR ADVENTURE

You are how almost ready to begin. You will start . by reading the PROLOGUE, and then proceed to **1**, and thence to further entries according to the decisions you make.

You may find it useful to take notes as you progress through the adventure. When you enter the pyramid, make a map of its rooms and passageways. If you get killed, fill in a new Character Sheet and start again, using your earlier maps and notes to guide you. It may take more than one attempt, but if you persevere you will eventually find a way past the Curse of the Pharaoh.

And now - your adventure begins . . .

PROLOGUE

Sweat trickles down your brow into your eyes, blinding you. The heat of the sun has bleached all colour from the land; all is a dazzling white. The horizon is a watery mirage where men and camels appear to walk not on sand but in mid-air. In front of you, minarets and towers, palm fronds and low buildings seem to hover in the dust-choked sky. The sun beats down on your head, seeming to boil your brains, and the metal of your sword burns with an intense white heat from where it hangs at your belt.

Two hundred miles you have travelled across the burning deserts of the land of Khem, following the caravan trains of the nomadic hawkers and merchants; in your belt a small slab of carved granite. It seems to have been half of a larger stone tablet judging by the rough edge down one of its sides. On it are the royal arms of a long-dead Pharaoh of this ancient land, Kharphut the Mighty. His tomb has been buried by the drifting desert sands for hundreds of years. This slab of stone, you hope, could be the first clue in finding it. The man who sold it to you told you it had been discovered near the city of Arkos, and told you the name of the dealer who he bought it off, one Gabbad, a merchant of antiquities. Many others have tried to find the tomb of this Lost Pharaoh, for mighty treasures were buried with him, but not only did they fail, they also all perished. Not one of them has been seen again striding back across the desert to the city of Arkos.

Finally, after miles of trudging during which the buildings you are approaching seem to recede from you, you wearily pass through the monolithic carved gates of the city. You are immediately surrounded by a crowd of excited children and beggars, some wear ragged cloaks, others are naked save flimsy loin cloths. They cry out, offering to take you to a good inn. You feel urgent hands tugging at your tunic. You brush past them, your eyes fixed upon the name carved over the entrance of a particularly shabby-looking inn just inside the city gate. The crowd fall back from you as you approach it; one of them calls out to you: 'Master, do not enter. That inn is accursed. There are many better ones in the city.' Ignoring their cries you enter the darkness of the Inn of the Coiled Serpent, eager to slake your thirst.

Your eyes gradually grow accustomed to the darkness. The inn has a dirt floor, and crude wooden tables and benches. Flies buzz in swarms around the earthenware pitchers and stale loaves behind the counter. A small, wizened old man with a fawning smile sidles out from behind the bar. You order some of the cool local beer and some food and sit down with it at one of the rough tables. The only other customer sits in a shadowy corner, his features obscured by one of the all-enveloping white cloaks of the desert nomads. After a while the innkeeper returns to remove your dish. You ask him where the shop of Gabbad the antiquarian dealer is. He pulls at a hair growing from one of his warts and looks at the ceiling, creasing the features of his face. 'Let me see now... let me see. The memory of an old man isn't what it used to be.' You toss a gold piece on to the table (cross it off your Character Sheet) and he snatches it up greedily.

'Aha! I've remembered now; his shop lies just off the bazaar. But hurry, for night is falling, and to be around the bazaar after nightfall is to be weary of one's life.'

You quickly hand over the few coins to pay for the meal and step out into the evening air. Ahead of you, you fancy you see the white-cloaked figure of the man in the inn slip through the gates of the city, apparently in a great hurry. You turn to your right and join the swearing mass of humanity crammed into the narrow streets of Arkos. Soon you reach the edge of the bazaar area. Your adventure begins here.

TURN TO **1**.

1

The last merchants are packing up their stalls as you enter the large open area of the bazaar. The remaining customers barge unceremoniously past you as you stand at the head of the alley, undecided what to do. The merchants seem too busy in their haste to answer your enquiries. The sky blushes a deep crimson as twilight settles. The only sounds are the excited shouts of a group of ragged children rushing around one corner of the square in wild circles.

In the distance a few country folk linger, gawping at the antics of a fire-eater who blows great gouts of flame into the darkening sky, throwing the spectators' faces into sudden relief. In another corner of the square, a group of rough looking men with scimitars in the belts of their robes lean against the wall of a small hut with the sign 'Gambling' outside the door. Immediately in front of you is a tavern where lanterns have already been lit, the lively music of the native drums and flutes echoes out into the square, and you hear shouting and clapping from within.

There is one stall left open. You can see a turbaned trader sitting in the shadows at the back of it smoking a long pipe. Unlike the other traders, he doesn't seem to be in a hurry to get out of the bazaar despite the coming darkness. You can dimly make out a number of items laid out on a carpet in front of him. Turn to **65**.

2

You take a sip of water, and feel refreshed, restore 2 VIGOUR points. Turn to **294**.

3

You fall backwards, landing with a sickening crunch on the hard pavement below. Lose 3 VIGOUR and 1 AGILITY. If you are still alive, you may either try to climb the wall with all your equipment again, turn to **67**, or you may leave it hidden in the shadows and try without it, turn to **24**.

4

You and Gabbad sit down on the old faded carpet. Suddenly it lifts into the air and you drift over the pass. You see a couple of hungry looking jaguars stalking around some human bones below you and you feel lucky that you had the foresight to buy the carpet. You notice that a thread of the carpet has become hitched to a bit of rock when, you laid it out and it is now unravelling at an alarming pace. You eventually bring it down when there, is hardly enough room for both of you to remain sitting on it. You have landed at the end of an avenue of stone sphinxes. In the distance you can see a small pyramid with a low building in front of it, and beyond that you can see a hill of sand rising up to the desert sky. The carpet has used up all its magic so you discard it. Cross it off your Character Sheet and turn to **56**.

5

The monster deflates like a burst balloon and oozes back into the sand. You grab the old man's arm and lead him back towards the pass. It looks like you are going to have to risk going through it. Turn to **36**.

6

It tells you that noon is the best time to enter the Tomb. If you want to ask the sphinx another question, pay another gold coin and turn back to **280**. Otherwise turn to **275**.

7

The sphinx tells you that the old man is in fact a ghost of a long-dead priest, sworn to the service of the demon Bos. Every year he lures a wandering stranger to accompany him to the pyramid of Kharphut the Mighty where he sacrifices them. It would seem that he has chosen you to be the sacrifice this year. If you would like to ask the sphinx another question, pay a gold coin and turn back to **280**. Otherwise, armed with this knowledge, turn to **275**.

8

Two energy bolts fly from the tip of your outstretched staff striking the demon. Black, noxious fumes escape from its wounds, but it keeps on coming at you. (The staff is now useless, cross it off your Character Sheet).

IPO: THE COILED SHADOWY HORROR
VIGOUR 12

Roll two dice:

score 2	The demon's darting tongue wraps around your face, its burning venom blinds you. Your adventure ends here.
score 3 to 7	It bites you; lose 4 VIGOUR.
score 8 to 12	The demon loses 3 VIGOUR.

If you win, turn to **93**.

9

The assassin falls to the ground, run through by your sword. You pick up his burning torch and hold it above your head. You are in an ancient granite vault. A corridor leads off to the north and you decide to explore it.

Turn to **283**.

10

The tribesman slopes off sulkily and you see him muttering in an angry fashion to some ruffians by the bar. They glare over in your direction, and you feel that it might be advisable to leave the inn as soon as possible. You step back into the square and look around. You decide that you will have to leave the area in case the tribesman and his friends are after your blood. You go over to the group of young children playing in the square to ask them for directions.

Turn to **190**.

11

The odds are better now that you have defeated one of the jaguars.

JAGUAR   VIGOUR 12

Roll two dice:
score 2 to 6   The jaguar strikes you; you
                     lose 3 VIGOUR
score 7 to 12   The jaguar loses 3 VIGOUR

If you win, turn to **68**.

12

It is almost noon as you enter the building and find yourself in a circular room. It is illuminated by a single beam of sunlight coming through a small opening in its domed ceiling. Paintings depicting the gods and demigods of Khem cover the walls. On a plinth in the centre of the room is a statue of an ancient pharaoh, a single gem set where his eyes should be. The beam of light from the ceiling is nearly glancing down directly on to the statue. If you want to look for secret doors in the walls, turn to **180**. If you would prefer to wait for a few minutes, turn to **50**.

13

You can't shrug off the fingers and you smell the thousand-year-old stale breath of a mummy on your face as he slowly bears you down to the floor of the room. Your adventure ends here.

14

You walk down to the end of the avenue of sphinxes and decide to investigate a low building you can see at the foot of the small pyramid. Suddenly Gabbad stumbles against you and falls to the ground. The heat has taken its toll on the old man and he has died of exhaustion. Sadly you bury him, but know you must continue with your task before you meet the same fate. You walk over to the building and enter through a low door. Turn to **35**.

15

You become increasingly nervous as you see the old man gliding closer and closer to where you are hiding in the shadows. Just as he is about to drift into the room that you are hiding in, however, the shaft of sunlight from the ceiling strikes the gem set into the face of the statue of the pharaoh. The whole room is suddenly illuminated by a blinding light. You notice that a panel has slid up in the wall near you and you step through the gap into the darkness. The panel clunks shut behind you. You light a torch and find yourself at the end of a long, rock-hewn passageway leading down in to the depths of the earth. Turn to **283**.

16

Gradually your vision swims back into focus and you find yourself lying in a room with your arms tied behind your back. Soon it stops spinning round. There are three men in front of you, one sitting cross-legged with an intent look on his face; the other two standing, their features obscured by black turbans pulled over their brows. They are armed with curved scimitars that are so huge that the men are leaning on them. The man sitting in front of you has thrown off his scarf and headdress and has rolled back the sleeves of his cloak, revealing two tattoos of coiled serpents on each of his forearms. He addresses you now that he sees you are conscious.

'So, stranger from the north, rumour has it that you are interested in finding the tomb of the Lost Pharaoh. What could have led you so far on such an obscure task? Maybe you have some sort of knowledge denied the people of Arkos for a thousand years or more? Speak, if you have any information that might be interesting to us; we will be merciful with you.'

Do you want to tell him everything you know about the tomb, and show him the tablet? If so, turn to **120**.

If you want to slip the tablet from your cloak and hide it behind you under the carpet, turn to **26**.

17

There is a large chamber at the end of the corridor. There are two exits in it, one to your left down a sloping passageway and one straight ahead of you across the room. Turn to **274**.

18

Your foot just catches one of the sculpted warriors as you land on the clear patch by the door. The figure you have knocked over suddenly starts to grow at an alarming rate: soon it is a full sized warrior clutching a sword. You must fight it.

SCULPTED WARRIOR   VIGOUR 9

Roll two dice:
score 2 to 6   The warrior hits you, you lose 3 VIGOUR
score 7 to 12   The warrior lose 3 VIGOUR

If you win, turn to **269**.

19

Your opponent is skilled and deadly. He circles you warily, twisting the blade of his sword so that it flashes in the torchlight.

THE BAZAAR SWORDSMAN   VIGOUR 9

Roll two dice:
score 2 to 7   He strikes you: you lose 3 VIGOUR
score 8 to 12   The swordsman loses 3 VIGOUR

If you win, turn to **259**.

20

There is something horribly eerie and sinister about the old man. You run in panic; in the distance you hear his sibilant whistling and you see him floating in the air in and out of the dunes, looking for you. He calls you by your name in a plaintive fashion. After a while you can no longer hear him. You realize that you're even more lost than you were before.
Roll a single die:

score 1 to 2   Turn to **182**
score 3 to 4   Turn to **232**
score 5 to 6   Turn to **39**

21

Which of the following, if you have them, would you like to use?

A potion of levitation: turn to **153**

A flying carpet: turn to **188**

If you have neither of these items, you will have to try running across the hall: turn to **177**

22

The water is cool and refreshing. As you soak in it, you feel all your wounds healing and your aches disappear as if a soothing balm had been applied to your skin. Your VIGOUR is restored to its *normal* score. After relaxing in the water a bit longer, you step out of the pool and continue on your way. Turn to **147**.

23

The odds are more favourable now that you have disposed of one of the jaguars.

JAGUAR   VIGOUR 12

Roll two dice:
score 2 to 6   The jaguar strikes you; you
                  lose 3 VIGOUR
score 7 to 12   The jaguar loses 3 VIGOUR

If you win, turn to **230**.

24

You pull off your backpack, and hide it behind a tree in the shadows. Cross off all the ITEMS on your Character Sheet apart from your sword, torch and the stone tablet. Now turn to **128**.

25

You pass through the mirror and find yourself in a large rectangular hall. A variegated pattern of light plays on its granite walls and ceilings. At the end of the hallway, you can see a broad staircase leading up to a landing. To the right of the staircase, you can see a doorway. There is something written over the lintel of the doorway.

If you would like to go up to the central staircase, turn to **256**.

If you would like to read what is written over the doorway, turn to **106**.

26

You slide the stone tablet under the thick rug on the floor. Looking the seated assassin in the eye, you tell him that he will not find the Lost Tomb without you. He glares at you angrily and orders his guards to search you. They find nothing on you. The leader looks extremely angry; but it now seems that he is going to have to make a deal with you. Turn to **102**.

27

Somehow you are back in the same room where you escaped from the old man. This time you are trapped, however. You see the distorted features of the demon Bos rise up from the shattered remains of the urn in the centre of the floor. He is eager to have his revenge on you for throwing him down in such an uncouth manner earlier on. Your adventure ends here.

28

Eventually Leon turns back to the table at which you are sitting; he seems rather surprised to see you still there. He smiles at you pleasantly, but you are beginning to suspect him of being treacherous. You feel you have no option, however, but to ask him where the house of Gabbad the merchant is, for it is getting late and you doubt whether you will be able to find anyone else to guide you. To your surprise, he readily agrees to take you there. You get up from your stool and go out into the square. Leon heads off down some dark alleyways: as a precaution you unsheath your sword and press it lightly to the back of his neck. He freezes immediately and you repeat your request to be lead to Gabbad's house. You are not surprised when he walks, somewhat reluctantly, back to the square and takes you down an entirely different route to the one you were being led down before.

Eventually he stops outside a darkened, shuttered house.

The front door has been barred for the night: to gain entry you will have to climb over the wall. You indicate to Leon that he should leave now, and he skulks off down the back alley.

You can either try to climb the wall with all your equipment, thus impairing your AGILITY (turn to **42**) or you may leave your equipment hidden by the wall and climb up without it (turn to **24**).

29

You pass along a corridor, eventually reaching a large chamber. There is an exit to your right, down a sloping passageway, and another one ahead of you across the room. Turn to **274**.

30

You aim the staff at the figures and there is a sudden bolt of blue lightning. When you look into the room, you see that all the figures have been vapourised. The staff has now got only one *energy bolt* left. Make a note of this next to your entry for the staff on your Character Sheet. You pass through the still smoking room to a banqueting chamber. An ancient feast was once laid out here, but all the food has withered into unappetising husks and a grey dust. You pass through the chamber, moving deeper into the tomb.

Turn to **62**.

31

You head over to a low building that you can see in front of the small pyramid. The heat is stifling: it is almost noon. Suddenly Gabbad stumbles against you and falls to the ground. The heat has taken its toll on the old man and he has died of exhaustion. Sadly you bury him, but know you must continue with your task before you meet the same fate. You enter the low building.

Turn to **12**.

As you reach your hand in, the gold coins vanish and are replaced by a nest of writing scorpions. If you are quick enough, you will be able to withdraw your hand before one of the arching stings of the scorpions strike at your hand.

Roll two dice, trying to roll equal to or less than your *current* AGILITY. If you succeed, turn to **98**. If you fail, turn to **82**.

The boy leads you off through some winding streets and up a steep flight of steps. You are just about to ask the boy whether he is sure where he is going when two black-robed figures wearing dark hoods leap out of a doorway and rush down the steps towards you. They whirl double-handed scimitars above their heads. You whip out your sword, preparing to take on both of them, but to your amazement the small boy sticks out a foot as one of them closes with you and the man trips and goes flying past you down the stairs. You hear a series of sickening bumps and the clatter of his sword as he tumbles down the near perpendicular steps behind you. You are left with only one opponent now.

ASSASSIN   VIGOUR 9

Roll two dice:
score 2 to 6   You are hit and lose 3 VIGOUR
score 7 to 12   The assassin loses 3 VIGOUR

If you win, turn to **195**.

It tells you that you will need the other half of the stone tablet, a magical rope and a glowing staff. If you would like to ask the sphinx another question, pay another gold coin and then turn back to **130**. Otherwise, turn to **14**.

35

You are in a circular room. It is illuminated by a single beam of light descending from a small hole set into a domed ceiling. At the centre of the room is a plinth with a stone statue representing one of the ancient pharaohs standing on it. A single gem has been set into the place where its eyes ought to be. There are a number of stylised representations of the gods of Khem painted on the walls. A number of skeletons lie around the floor. They are clad in armour and clutch weapons in their bony hands. They have been riddled by arrows.

Do you want to look for a secret exit from this room? If so, turn to **180**.

Or do you want to wait for a few minutes and see what happens when the beam of light hits the statue at midday? If so, turn to **176**.

36

You notice that there are a number of human skeletons lying in the rocky gorge. You set off cautiously down it. Suddenly you hear a low animal growl, and there is a blur of movement ahead of you. You see two swiftly moving jaguars heading towards you over the rocks. Have you a Potion of Swiftness? If you have, turn to **77**. If you haven't, you will have to fight: turn to **125**.

37

You look around you and find that you have no idea where the city is anymore: your guide has got you totally lost. You sit down despondently on a dune. Tomorrow the sun will rise and you will die within a few hours as you don't have any water. Then, incredibly, you hear the sound of a tuneless whistling, and you see a thin, gaunt man, dressed in an antique leopard skin cloak, moving gracefully towards you over the dunes. Do you want to wait for him (turn to **88**) or would you prefer to avoid him (turn to **20**)?

38

You decide it isn't worth betting as the money you have will be enough to pay off the old man. Setting your teeth into a grim smile you enter the arena of human bodies, your hand clenched on your sword.

Turn to **19**.

39

You trudge on and on over the interminable dunes. Soon the sun rises and with it comes the baking heat of the day. Do you have any water? If you don't, you lose 3 VIGOUR through thirst. If you survive, turn to **46**.

40

Despite your caution, you step on to a hidden panel on the floor. Suddenly a section of the wall swings round at you, a serried row of sharp metal stakes attached to it. You are impaled by them before you can move. Your adventure ends here.

41

You drop the pot on to the stone floor. The old man howls as if in terrible pain as you do so. To your satisfaction, you see him suddenly vanish. Looking down you see a noxious cloud of vapour emanating from the shattered fragments of the pot. This materializes into the shape of a hideous green-hued demon. It smacks it lips when it sees you. You have no power to fight against it. Your adventure ends here.

42

Climbing the wall with all your equipment proves to be rather awkward. Just as you get to the top of the wall, your backpack snags on some foliage causing you to teeter precariously. Roll two dice, trying to roll equal to or less than your *current* AGILITY. If you succeed, turn to **63**. If you fail, turn to **3**.

43

The boulder rolls past the alcove in the wall and lodges with a loud grating noise further down the passageway where it narrows. You now cannot go back. You climb the remaining steps.

Turn to **229**.

44

You slip and fall under the remorselessly advancing boulder. It rolls over you crushing you flat: your adventure ends here.

45

Have you got *either* an unused Flying Carpet (turn to **213**) *or* a Potion of Levitation (turn to **135**)? If not, you must try to jump (turn to **254**).

46

You sight the city at about noon. You stumble through the gates and drink greedily from a fountain. Then you slump into an exhausted slumber by a wall. When you wake up, it is evening. You decide that it is no good trusting the local tribesmen to lead you to the tomb of the Lost Pharaoh; you will have to seek out the house of Gabbad, the merchant of antiquities. You go to the bazaar and walk up to a group of children you see playing there, intending to ask them the way.

Turn to **190**.

47

The ghost disappears with a wail of disappointment. Turn to **261**.

48

You leave the room, cat calls and shrieks of mocking laughter following you. You emerge back into the bazaar. Do you want to go and talk to the children who are still playing in the corner of the square (turn to **190**), go and join the crowd looking at the fire-eater (turn to **210**), or go to the inn (turn to **123**)?

49

After two days travel in the desert, you pass down a narrow stony gorge and emerge in front of a small pyramid. You can see an oasis away in the distance and an avenue of stone sphinxes. Your captors lead you into a small building in front of the pyramid. Peering in, you see a circular room illuminated by a small hole set into the domed ceiling of the building. A thin shaft of sunlight angles down from it, striking the floor to the right of a stone plinth at the centre of the room. There is a small statue of some ancient Pharaoh on the plinth, a single gem set where its eyes should be. The walls are painted with stylised representations of the gods of Khem: you see pictures of a jackal-headed man, a woman with cow's horns and a solar disc atop her head, a bearded man holding the crook and mitre of one of the old Pharaohs and many others deities and demigods. The eyes of the paintings are at the same height as the head of the statue. A number of skeletons lie on the sandy floor: they wear armour and their weapons are still in their hands. Their bodies are riddled with arrows. The leader of the assassins looks at you expectantly, obviously waiting for you to do something. You feel the bonds around your wrists being cut. It is nearly noon and the shaft of sunlight from the ceiling hovers over the statue on the plinth.

Do you want to start searching the walls for a secret doorway? If so, turn to **110**.

If you would prefer to wait until noon, despite the growing impatience of the leader, turn to **155**.

50

Soon the sun strikes the gem at the centre of the statue's forehead giving off a blinding, incandescent light. Through the glare you can just manage to see a panel slide up in the wall near you. You step through the opening and light a torch. You find yourself at the end of a long granite corridor descending, it would seem, into the depths of the earth. Turn to **283**.

51

The snake bites you on your arm; you lose 3 VIGOUR points. It falls to the floor and wriggles away into a small crevice in the wall. If you are still alive, turn to **146**.

52

As you approach the staff a tremendous bolt of energy leaps out at you from it. Roll two dice, trying to roll equal to or less than your *current* PSI. If you succeed, turn to **206**. If you fail, turn to **295**.

53

You continue down the passageway to a right-hand bend. Just before you reach the bend, you hear a loud clacking noise, and a huge beetle, clicking its hideous horny mandibles at you, lurches around the corner of the corridor, completely blocking it. Just as you are about to turn and flee, a stone block slides down, blocking the corridor behind you. You are now trapped and will have to fight the hideous creature.

GIANT BEETLE   VIGOUR 15

Roll two dice:

score 2	You are seized in the creatures mandibles, its horny mouth closes over your head and your adventure ends here.
score 3 to 6	The creature's jaws tear your arm; you lose 3 VIGOUR
score 7 to 12	You hit the creature, it loses 3 VIGOUR

If you win, turn to **64**.

54

You shrug off the effect of the music which was lulling you into a dream trance from which you would never have awoken. The music fades from your ears and you hurriedly vacate the room by a door you see at the other side. Turn to **90**.

55

The waiter starts shouting abuse at you when he realizes that you have no money. He angrily pushes you towards the door and you stumble out into the square.

You can try going back to the inn (turn to **285**) or you can go across to the children playing in the square (turn to **190**).

56

One of the sphinxes is particularly interesting. It stands two metres high and has strange hieroglyphic signs carved on its chest. There is a stone offering bowl between its leonine paws. You can see a number of gold coins inside the offering bowl.

Do you want to reach in and pull out some of the gold coins? If so, turn to **76**.

If you'd prefer to throw one gold coin into the bowl (if you have one) turn to **130**.

If you would prefer to ignore the sphinx, turn to **31.**

57

Twisting round you see your assailant towering over you. Before you stands a large leonine being caked in white dust. It has taloned claws, a flowing mane and a semi-human face and body. It is holding a wickedly curved knife in one of its paws. In its other paw, it has a fresh human heart. You must fight it.

THE EATER OF HEARTS   VIGOUR 15

Roll two dice:

score 2	The creature stretches out one of its clawed paws and rips the heart from your body. You are killed instantly.
score 3 to 6	You are wounded by the creature; you lose 3 VIGOUR
score 7 to 12	The Eater of Hearts loses 3 VIGOUR

If you defeat the creature, turn to **186**.

58

The corridor starts to spin and everything becomes cloudy in your mind. You feel yourself being conveyed somewhere magically. Turn to **288**.

You hand the money to the old man who grunts in satisfaction, weighing the gold in his hand. 'Let us talk then,' he says - he gestures you through to a lamp-lit room at the back of the house. You sit and watch him intently as he relates his tale.

'As I have said, I remember this stone, and it would seem that it remembers me, by the way the accursed thing has found its way back to me just when I looked forward to spending my last few years in peace and tranquility. Yet it is not to be, it would seem; at least your gold will be some comfort to my nephew here if I should perish.' He indicates the young boy sitting on a stool nearby.

'Ten years ago I sold the stone to a nomadic trader. By then I had lost both my wife and my apprentice through its evil ministry, and my shop had been broken into and ransacked a number of times.' He falls silent, lost in memory. After a while he continues, 'It was curious how Aktan, my apprentice and I found the stone. We had been looking for antiquities near the Great Necropolis in the desert for a week but without success. We decided to move further to the West into the emptiness of the Lost Quarter; even the nomads fear to go there, but we were younger then, and carefree. We wandered for a day or two. Suddenly we spotted a figure ahead lying in the sand. How that man had crawled anywhere I will never understand: every bone in his body had been shattered by some terrible accident, yet somehow he was still alive. He muttered in his delirium of how he had dared the Pharaoh's curse, yet he had failed because he lacked the other half of this stone. He died soon afterwards. Aktan and I followed his blood soaked trail in the sand for over a mile. We had just sighted a large hill standing up from the dunes a mile in front of us when out of nowhere a blinding sandstorm engulfed us. I never saw Aktan again. The storm kept up for two days and nights. Eventually I stumbled back here half-dead, blabbing my story to all who cared to hear. Soon afterwards, as I said, my shop was broken into and my wife foully murdered. I blamed it all on the stone, and so sold it.

'Sure enough, my life has been untroubled up to this hour; then I hear a fight in my courtyard, and (the Pharaoh will have his vengeance!) who should it be fighting with my servant but he who has bought back the wretched stone. I am old now and would like to die peacefully, but I know this will never be now. Tomorrow, then, let us go to the desert and solve this mystery once and for all. I will guide you to the Lost Quarter, your gold thus far is adequate payment. Meanwhile rest on this couch, we will depart early tomorrow morning.'

He indicates a sleeping pallet. You lie down and doze off surprisingly quickly. Turn to **297**.

60

You walk down the causeway, the crocodiles snapping up at you from the water with their pink jaws. Just before you get to the statues, you edge out to one side. Just as you draw level with one of them, and are teetering over the edge of the crocodile-filled pool, one of the statue's massive arms swings round at you. You are going to have to dodge it, or else be knocked into the pool. Roll two dice, trying to roll equal to or less than your *current* AGILITY, If you succeed, turn to **215**. If you fail, turn to **212**.

61

It tells you that you must go to the shrine room in front of the small pyramid. If you would like to ask the sphinx another question, pay another gold coin and turn back to **130**. Otherwise, turn to **14**.

62

Leaving the banqueting hall, you move into a bathroom covered with intricately painted tiles. You can see an exit at the other side of the room. There is a huge pool filled with water in the centre of the room. Steps lead down into it and a curious green light seems to burn at the bottom of it. Looking in, you see the symbol of the Pharaoh carved on to the pool's stone bottom.

Would you like to wade into the pool? If you do, turn to **22**.

If you would prefer to continue, ignoring the pool, turn to **147**.

63

You just manage to avoid falling backwards into the alleyway. You wipe the sweat from your brow and drop down into a paved courtyard. A fountain bubbles away merrily at its centre, and the night wind sighs gently in the cypress trees that stand in the corners. Suddenly you sense a presence creeping up on you from the shadows and you swing to face an assailant armed with a club. Your assailant will surrender if you wound him *twice.*

SHADOWY ASSAILANT   VIGOUR 9

Roll two dice:
score 2 to 6   You are hit; lose 3 VIGOUR
score 7 to 12   Your opponent loses 3 VIGOUR

If you wound him twice, turn to **300**.

64

You step over the remains of the beetle. It exudes a pale brown liquid where your sword has broken its carapace. You reach the bend in the corridor. Looking down to the right, you can see two doors covered with gold foil: they give off a beautiful reflection in your torchlight. You approach the doors, seeing on them the seal of the Lost Pharaoh, Kharphut the Mighty. You push open the doors, and step into the Pharaoh's tomb chamber.

Turn to **242**.

You stroll up to the stall. A sign hangs from its awning: 'Ahmed's Emporium'. There is a flash of white teeth as the trader smiles in the blackness of the stall.

'Greetings, warrior from the north. Tonight I have a choice selection of articles.' Ignoring the cheap trinkets laid out on the carpet in front of him, he brings out a mouldered old carpet, much frayed at the edges. He unravels it, revealing an assortment of articles.

'All these are excellent bargains, noble sir. This pair of gloves are strong enough to keep you safe from the bites of snakes - a mere 5 Gold pieces. And this Potion of Levitation will enable you to drift through the air at a height of 1 metre above the ground - again, a bargain at 5 Gold pieces. This water bottle always has at least one gulp of water in it.'

He pours water in at the top of the bottle but the water quickly dribbles out of the bottom as if it was riddled with holes. After this flow has stopped, he triumphantly reverses the bottle and a small amount of water pours out of its spout. 'See!' he exclaims. 'A wondrous device - and a mere five gold pieces. And here I have two potions of swiftness: these will enable you to escape a deadly foe - for only two gold pieces each. Finally, a bargain that even you cannot refuse - a genuine flying carpet! Admittedly, it has only one hour's flying time left in it, but I am selling it at the bargain price of five gold pieces.'

If you would like to buy any or all of these articles, you may hand over the money and add the articles to the items listed on your Character Sheet. Then you turn to look at the other things in the Bazaar.

If you want to risk some gambling to improve your funds, turn to **218**. Otherwise, do you want to go over and speak to the group of children playing in the corner of the square (turn to **190**), join the group of people staring at the fire-eater (turn to **210**), or cross the square and investigate the inn (turn to **123**)?

66

You push open the heavy door in front of you and enter an ancient banqueting hall. You bar the door behind you, and go and inspect the table. Hundreds of years ago it must have been set for a banquet; crockery and wooden spoons and forks are laid out in front of ornate seats. Unfortunately the food laid out on serving dishes and in fruit bowls has all withered, so there is no longer anything but a few dried husks. Your stomach is beginning to crave for food.

Do you have a gold medallion? If you do, turn to **265**. If you don't, turn to **203**.

67

Despite your fall, you don't want to leave any equipment behind you. You manage to get to the top of the wall again, but again overbalance. Roll two dice, trying to roll less than or equal to your *current* AGILITY. If you succeed, turn to **63**. If you fail, turn to **3**.

68

The old man is waiting for you at the end of the rocky gorge. He congratulates you on your victory. 'They didn't seem to be interested in my old bones,' he says, chuckling in an eerie manner. You are becoming rather suspicious, but decide to trudge after him over the burning sand. Turn to **236**.

69

You throw the urn on to the floor, shattering it. You dive towards the rapidly closing door. Roll two dice, trying to score equal to or less than your *current* AGILITY. If you succeed, turn to **157**. If you fail, turn to **86**.

70

The carved stone skull stares down at you as you pass under the lintel of the right-hand door. There is a straight stone passageway leading to the north ahead of you. A feeling of dread comes over you but you manage to shrug it off and walk down the corridor. Do you have a complete stone tablet with the Pharaoh's symbol on it? If you do, turn to **154.** If you don't, turn to **40.**

71

You pick up the eye gingerly. Suddenly you experience a strange feeling of dislocation - the crystal eye has come alive, and you can see through it, even though you are holding it in the palm of your hand! You experiment a bit, and find that the crystal operates as a third eye. You can use it to look up, sideways, behind you or any other way while your own eyes are looking in a different direction. In addition to the eye, you find a tumbler with a dice in it. All its sides are marked with six dots. Note this down on your Character Sheet if you would like to take it.

Where do you want to put the eye:

Do you want to fasten it to the front of your cloak? Turn to **291**.

To the back of your cloak? Turn to **201**.

Or do you want to drop it into your backpack? Turn to **185**.

72

The corridor bends to the right. Eventually it leads to an empty stone chamber. Just as you are crossing it, you hear the clicking sound of ivory dice being rolled. Looking round, you see that a skeletal apparition has materialized in the centre of the room. The clicking sound is being made as it tosses a dice from its bony hand on to the floor. Do you want to run for the entrance on the far side of the room (turn to **162**), or do you want to stop and hear what the apparition wants from you (turn to **194**)?

73

Do you have a magical rope? If you do, turn to **141**. If you don't, turn to **286**.

74

You pick up the goblet and an apple. Immediately the apple turns into a writhing snake in your hand, and a poisonous gas rises up from the goblet and into your face. Roll one die:

score 1 to 2	Turn to **228**
score 3 to 4	Turn to **117**
score 5 to 6	Turn to **251**

75

A corridor leads away from the archway to the left. You walk along it for a while and then enter an empty room. Suddenly you hear the sound of ghostly flutes, and the shapes of ghostly musicians materialize out of the dust in the corner of the room. They play a sweet dance tune of a bygone age. You feel that you would like to remain here forever listening to it.

Do you have an ornate flute? If you do, turn to **163**. If you don't, turn to **243**.

76

As you reach forward your hand, the gold coins vanish and are replaced by a nest of writhing scorpions. If you are quick enough, you will be able to withdraw your hand before it is stung. Roll two dice, trying to roll equal to or less than your *current* AGILITY. If you succeed, turn to **250**. If you fail, turn to **264**.

77

How many Potions of Swiftness do you have? If you have two, you give one to Gabbad. Turn to **293**. If you have only one, turn to **196**.

78

You are pushed back down the corridor until you are being crushed against the stone wall behind you. It is now extremely difficult for you to jab at it with your sword because of the confined space.

Roll two dice:

score 2	Slowly the worm's jaws close around you and you are sucked down its moist throat. Your adventure ends here.
score 3 to 7	You are crushed against the wall. You lose 3 VIGOUR
score 8 to 12	You manage to hit the worm; it loses 3 VIGOUR

If you win, turn to **299**.

79

You pick up the sceptre and the half of the stone tablet. You fit the stone fragment to the bit you already have: they are a perfect match. You hold the sceptre up, admiring it in the torchlight; then it suddenly vanishes into thin air. You notice that the ghost of the Pharaoh too has disappeared, as has the table with the sword on it. Suddenly the gold ornament over the throne swings back revealing a secret passageway. Turn to **103**.

80

The other crocodiles turn on the one you have beaten in combat, rending it to pieces with their hideous jaws. You take the opportunity to paddle like mad for the platform. You step up on to the safety of the platform, and watch as the crocodiles finish off their former companion.

Do you now want to inspect the casket on top of the pyramid? If you do, turn to **174**.

If you would prefer to skirt around the pyramid and walk over the other causeway to the arch in the west wall, turn to **249**.

You are almost deafened as you enter the inn, a wave of feverish drum music washes over you and you are half-blinded by the thick haze of smoke that wafts out of the door. You see a small stage set up at the far end of the room where a band of turbaned drummers are ecstatically accompanying the movements of a veiled belly-dancer. Leon leads you right through the throng of drinkers to a table by the stage. You sit down with him and he orders two drinks. To your surprise, the waiter asks *you* for the money for them. Do you have the one gold piece he is asking for? If you do, turn to **133**. If you don't, turn to **55**.

82

One of the scorpions flicks its tail and strikes your exposed hand before you have time to withdraw it. You feel poison coursing through your veins. You lose 6 VIGOUR points. If you are still alive, turn to **275**.

83

The monster towers over you, its ghastly maw stretched open, waiting to rend you into a thousand pieces with its razor-sharp incisors.

OASIS MONSTER   VIGOUR 15

Roll two dice:

score 2	The monster swallows you whole; your adventure ends here.
score 3 to 6	The monster catches you with its sharp teeth; you lose 3 VIGOUR
score 7 to 12	You hit the monster and it loses 3 VIGOUR

If you win, turn to **5**.

84

The corridor soon bends to the north again and you walk for a while down a gaudily painted passageway. Eventually it turns at right-angles, to the west. Just at the angle of the corridor, on the north wall, you can see that the plasterwork has been chipped away at head height, leaving a small hole.

If you would like to take a look through the hole, turn to **161**.

If you would prefer to continue down the corridor to the west, turn to **193**.

85

There is a stone carved relief over the right-hand archway. It shows a room filled with musicians playing flutes. Warriors cavort in front of them in a grotesque mimicry of dance. If you would like to pass under the archway, turn to **75**. If you would prefer to inspect the left-hand archway, turn to **197**.

86

You dive for the small gap between the descending block and the floor but it is coming down too fast, and you are caught only halfway through it. Remorselessly the block keeps descending, crushing the life from your body. Your adventure ends here.

You whip out your sword and the hubbub in the inn gradually subsides; all eyes are on you as you point the tip of it at Leon and his friend. They swing round, pushing over the table between you and drawing wickedly curved daggers. You are going to have to fight them together.

LEON   VIGOUR 6
PICKPOCKET   VIGOUR 6

Roll two dice:

score 2 to 3	Both of them stab you at the same time; you lose 6 VIGOUR
score 4 to 6	One of them breaks your guard and you are stabbed; lose 3 VIGOUR
score 7 to 12	One of them (of your choice) loses 3 VIGOUR

If your VIGOUR points' total drops to under 6, you have been overpowered and thrown out into the square, turn to **144**. If you kill one of them, turn to **253**.

The old man stops in front of you. He has a very pale complexion, and hollow sunken eye sockets. 'You seek the tomb of Kharphut the Mighty, the Lost Pharaoh,' he states in a sibilant voice. 'I can lead you to it in return for a small favour. As you can see, I am a weak old man.' He holds out frail, reed-like arms. 'You must carry that urn to the tomb for me.'

He points to an urn half-buried in the sand by your feet. You didn't notice it there before. Still, you realize that you are in a bad position and need all the help you can get, so you pick up the urn and set off after the old man.

Turn to **298**.

89

You flee back down the corridor: the boulder is gaining on you every second. Roll two dice, trying to score equal to or less than your *current* AGILITY. If you succeed, turn to **208**. If you fail, turn to **44**.

90

The long corridor starts to lead upwards. Eventually you come to a junction. You may turn left (turn to **17**) or go straight on through *a* doorway ahead of you which has a carved skull over the lintel (turn to **70**).

91

It tells you that you must go to the small shrine room, with a domed ceiling and painted walls, in front of the small pyramid. If you would like to ask the sphinx another question, pay another gold coin and turn back to **280**. Otherwise, turn to **275**.

92

It tells you that you will need the other half of the stone tablet, a magical rope, and a glowing staff. If you would like to ask the sphinx another question, pay another gold coin and turn back to **280**. Otherwise, turn to **275**.

93

Your final blow slices through the scaly carcass of the demon and suddenly it is no longer there. You hear a low whistling noise, quite similar to the one you heard when it arrived, receding into the distance. There is no trace of the body of the demon. Wearily, you start to climb up the ramp to the platform. At the top of the ramp there is a hollow altar stone. Looking into it you see a nest of writhing snakes surrounding a lever set into the stone. A narrow passageway ascends steeply in front of you. There are arched exits to either end of the platform.

Do you want to see if you can reach the lever amongst the snakes? If so, turn to **258**.

If you would like to go up the steep ascending passageway in front of you, turn to **240**.

If you would like to go through the right-hand archway, turn to **85**.

If you would like to go through the left-hand archway, turn to **197**.

94

The corridor finishes in a dead end just in front of the figure. There is a rough rock face, with baskets full of rubble, and picks and adzes littered around as if the workmen had only recently abandoned their attempts to lengthen the tunnel. In actuality many hundreds of years have passed since they were last here. The figure is dressed in dusty robes. A number of jagged knives protrude from his blood-soaked back. One of his arms is outstretched. Next to it you can see an ornate ivory flute; it seems to have broken in two halves when the man fell. However, when you pick it up (note it down as an item on your Character Sheet) you see that it is designed to screw back together again. You do so and play it. You hear a haunting tune. Do you have the magical rope? If you do turn to **171**. If you don't, turn to **287**.

95

Deadly poison spreads into your veins from the bite. Within seconds you feel dizzy and stagger to and fro, eventually blacking out. You do not recover. Your adventure ends here.

96

Leon doesn't notice you slipping the contents of the phial into his drink. He takes a large gulp out of it and turns to say something to you. Suddenly his eyes glaze over and he collapses across the table snoring loudly. Looking up, you see the belly-dancer wink at you. Curious people are now staring at you from other tables and you decide that it would be a good time to leave. You go outside and find yourself back in the bazaar square.

From where you stand in the shadows you see Leon stumble out of the inn and look around him angrily. He is holding his head as if he has a terrible hangover. Obviously the contents of the phial were not to his liking! If you would like to slip back into the inn, turn to **123**. Or would you rather go and talk to the children playing in the corner of the square? Turn to **190**.

97

Just as you reach the edge of the water, you notice that it is not water at all, but some strange ectoplasm. Looking down into its depths, you see a hideous face with hundreds of eyes and thousands of razor-sharp teeth staring up at you. The ground around you begins to heave and suddenly the monster bursts upwards, scattering trees and skeletons all around you.

This is going to be the toughest fight of your life. You will only be able to FLEE if you have a potion of swiftness. If you have one such potion and want to use it, leaving Gabbad behind, turn to **107**.

If you have two such potions and want to give one of them to Gabbad to drink, turn to **115.**

If you want to try fighting the monster, turn to **83**.

98

You just manage to pull your hand away in time. Deciding that you have had enough of the sphinx, you rejoin the old man who is waiting for you at the end of the avenue. Turn to **275**.

99

You are led on through the burning dunes, your captors never slackening in their long strides. After a couple of hours, you notice a group of nomads sitting astride some camels at the top of a nearby dune. They seem even fiercer than they did in the city. You realize that it might work to your advantage if you could provoke an argument between them and your captors.

You could drop the stone tablet, and hope that the nomads will see you do so and follow you out of curiosity. If you would like to do so, turn to **140**. If you would prefer to keep the slab, turn to **49**.

100

You point the tip of the staff towards the demon. Three times bolts of bright blue lightning flash from its tip, each time striking the advancing demon, and causing it to smoke dark noxious fumes. Nevertheless it is still alive when it reaches you, although badly damaged. (The staff is now useless, cross it off your Character Sheet).

IPO: THE COILED SHADOWY HORROR
VIGOUR 6

Roll two dice:

score 2	The demon's darting tongue wraps itself round your face, its burning venom blinding you. It has no trouble finishing you off now. Your adventure ends here.
score 3 to 7	You are bitten by the demon; you lose 4 VIGOUR
score 8 to 12	You hit the demon; it loses 3 VIGOUR

If you win, turn to **93**.

101

You leap for the centre of the room. Roll two dice, trying to roll equal to or less than your *current* AGILITY. If you succeed, turn to **204**. If you fail, turn to **244**.

102

The leader looks at you. 'Tomorrow you will guide us to the Lost Tomb,' he says. He clicks his fingers and the guards tie you even more securely. They leave the room taking the lamp with them. You are now in darkness. You have just got room to move your hands underneath the carpet and recover the stone slab.

Turn to **282**.

103

You duck under the low stone portal in front of you, finding yourself in a low corridor covered with finely painted hieroglyphics. There is an opening at the end of the corridor from which comes a golden radiance. You realize you are on the threshold of the tomb of Kharphut the Mighty, the Lost Pharaoh. Stooping, you walk down to the end of the passageway and look into the burial chamber.

Turn to **242**.

104

You rush off down the slope, the weight of the urn not exactly aiding your escape. Eventually you reach the shadows of the entrance to the low building you noticed in front of the pyramid. Peering out, you see the old man gliding down towards your hiding place, his sunken eyes ablaze with hatred. You look around the circular room you are in. It is illuminated by a single beam of light descending from a small hole set into its domed ceiling. At the centre of the room is a plinth with a stone statue of one of the ancient pharaohs resting on it. A single gem has been set into the place where its eyes ought to be. There are a number of stylised representations of the gods of Khem painted on the walls. A group of skeletons lie around the walls; they wear leather armour and still clutch weapons in their bony hands. The skeletons have been riddled by a number of arrows. Looking out again, you see the old man gliding backwards and forwards looking for you and calling you by your name.

Do you want to look for a secret exit from this room (turn to **180**), or do you want to wait until midday, which can't be far off (turn to **15**)?

105

This stone was apparently found by you somewhere in the desert. I believe that you must have discovered it somewhere near the location of the Lost Tomb of the Pharaoh, Kharphut the Mighty.' You hold the stone up for the old man to look at. He surveys it through rheumy eyes, and nods his head slowly.

'Aye, I remember this stone. I sold it to a nomadic trader ten, or maybe twelve years ago. I suspected even then that it might have magical powers, that it was accursed. My apprentice died on the trip that discovered it, and not long after my wife was butchered by assassins in the street. After that my shop was constantly broken into and ransacked. I decided to get rid of the stone as soon as possible. Sure enough, my sorrows soon ended. Now you have brought it back to me, and by doing so have brought back all my bitter memories.'

There is a silence as the old man casts back in his mind, reliving the past. 'It was curious how my apprentice Aktan, may he rest in peace, and I found the stone. We had been looking for antiquities near the Great Necropolis in the desert for over a week without success. We decided to move further to the West into the emptiness of the Lost Quarter where not even the nomads go. We wandered about in the area for a day or so. Suddenly we spotted a figure ahead lying in the sand. How that man had crawled anywhere I will never know. Every bone in his body seemed to have been fractured, yet he was still alive. He muttered in his delirium of how he had dared to risk the Lost Pharaoh's curse, yet he had failed because he lacked the other half of this stone. He died soon afterwards. My apprentice and I, our greed excited by the rich rewards we knew awaited anyone who discovered the tomb, followed the man's blood-stained trail through the sand for about a mile. We saw a large hill in the distance but then, out of nowhere, a sandstorm engulfed us. I never saw Aktan again. The storm kept up for two days and nights. Half-dead through thirst I eventually stumbled back into the town, stupidly blabbing out my story. Evil men heard it, I am sure, hence my miserable existence for the months that followed. Eventually in my despair I sold the stone to a passing merchant. I hadn't thought of the accursed thing for years.'

Gabbad looks at you. 'I am old now,' he says, 'and have nothing to live for. My brother, this boy's father, will look after the shop. I will come with you through the desert tomorrow and act as your guide. If I do so, maybe I will at last lay to rest the ghosts of my poor wife and the unfortunate Aktan. Who knows? We must act fast though, rival groups in the town have probably heard of your arrival. Believe me, they will stop at nothing to obtain this stone.'

You tell him of your recent narrow escape and he looks at you darkly, shaking his head. He gives you a meal of fruits and wine and then shows you to a sleeping pallet laid on the floor.

Turn to **297**.

106

Although it is written in the ancient tongue of Khem, you manage to decipher the message written over the door; it reads: 'Enter here and conquer thyself.'

If you wish to enter the room, turn to **252**. If you would prefer to go up the central staircase, turn to **256**.

107

You quickly drink the contents of the phial and rush swiftly across the sands. You hear Gabbad's screams as he is consumed by the monster and feel a slight pang of guilt. You don't stop running for quite some time, and you feel very thirsty. Have you any water? If you have, turn to **237**. If you haven't turn to **272**.

108
The apparition rolls its die, scoring a four. Roll one die, trying to score equal to or more than this roll. If you succeed, turn to **47**. If you fail, turn to **278**.

109
You run off, stumbling under the weight of the urn. The jaguars are right behind you; you pass the old man who is still strolling on nonchalantly. Suddenly you feel a tearing pain as the first jaguar catches up with you, and rakes its claws down your back. You lose 3 VIGOUR. If you are still alive, turn to **284**.

110
You step over the skeletons on the floor and begin to grope around on the walls looking for a hidden doorway. Suddenly your hand pushes a concealed panel and there is a sudden hissing sound. A flight of arrows hurtles out of the far wall thudding into your body. Black waves of unconsciousness overwhelm you. Your adventure ends here.

111

Your foot lands on an area of the floor which suddenly gives way. You fall down a rubble filled chute, choked with dust and ancient skeletons. You eventually come to rest with a bone shattering impact against a fallen column somewhere deep inside the heart of the pyramid. Looking up, you see the hideous leering face of a crocodile-headed demon bending over your helpless body. Your adventure ends here.

112

Your sword goes right through the tribesman, and he expires with a blood-curdling gurgle. You recover your two Gold pieces from his body (note them on your Character Sheet). You then look around you, trying to establish where you are. Turn to **37**.

113

After an hour or so, you find yourself at the end of an avenue of sphinxes. One of the sphinxes is particularly interesting. It is two metres high and has strange hieroglyphics carved on its chest. There is a stone offering bowl between its paws. You look in and see a number of gold coins in it.

If you have got a gold coin and want to throw it into the offering bowl, turn to **130**. If you would like to ignore it and pass down the avenue of sphinxes, turn to **31**.

114

You now seem to have no other options, apart from going to talk to the group of children on the other side of the square. Turn to **190**.

115

You quickly throw one of the potions to Gabbad, drinking one yourself. Suddenly you feel as if you can run as swiftly as a gazelle and you turn on your heels and bolt across the desert at lightning speed. To your amazement, the old man can keep up with you. You soon leave the monster far behind. You eventually find yourself at the end of an avenue of sphinxes standing next to a small pyramid in the middle of the desert. There is a large hill behind the pyramid in the background. Gabbad recognizes this as the place that he and his apprentice saw many years before when they followed the blood-soaked trail through the desert. Turn to **56**.

116

You continue to wander about the desert, but soon realize that without Gabbad you are horribly lost. Eventually night falls and you sit disconsolately on a dune, knowing that tomorrow the heat of the sun will probably finish you off, even if the savage monsters of the Lost Quarter don't. Suddenly you hear a strange whistling sound, and looking up, you see an old man dressed in an antique leopard skin cloak striding towards you over the dunes.

'Hail stranger,' he says. 'I know you have come afar to seek out the tomb of the Lost Pharaoh, Kharphut the Mighty. I will lead you to that tomb, if you will grant me the boon of carrying that urn for me.'

You look down at your feet and see an urn half-buried in the sand: you hadn't noticed it before. You readily agree to the old man's request. He sets off across the sand at a brisk pace and you find it difficult to keep up with him. You wonder how long you will be able to keep up the pace. Turn to **298**.

117

Do you have a snake bite proof glove, bought from Ahmed's Emporium? If you do, turn to **152**. If you haven't got one, turn to **51**.

118

It tells you that noon is the best time to enter the tomb. If you would like to ask the sphinx another question, pay another gold coin and then turn back to **130**. Otherwise, turn to **14**.

119

You leave the tavern in a hushed and sinister silence. You feel that at any moment a knife will be flung at your back or someone will call after you. You make it out into the street however. Do you now want to go and talk to the children playing in the corner of the square (turn to **190**), or go and join the crowd looking at the fire-eater (turn to **210**)?

120

You hold up the slab that you were concealing in your cloak. One of the guards steps forward and wrenches it from your grasp, handing it to the man sitting on the ground. He looks at it, a gleam of triumph in his eyes. Abruptly he gestures to the guards to come over and pick you up. You are still too groggy from the drug to react. They take you to a trapdoor and throw you down it. You land heavily. In the darkness you hear the hiss of a thousand snakes all around you and slithering objects begin to worm in and out of your clothing, biting your flesh with their poisonous fangs. Your adventure ends here.

You manage to shrug off the numbing tiredness that was weighing on you. Do you still want to confront Leon and his pickpocket friend? If you do, turn to **87**. If you are prepared to ignore Leon's apparent friendliness with this thief, turn to **28**.

You unfurl the flying carpet and step on to it. It lifts off into the air, and glides smoothly over the heads of the statues to the other side of the room. You open the heavy oak door and glide into what must have at one time been a banqueting hall. The shrivelled remains of bits of meat testify to a meal that was set hundreds of years before. The carpet is now useless, so cross it off your Character Sheet. You move on to the next chamber. Turn to **62**.

You walk up to the entrance of the inn and push aside the bead hangings that cover the doorway. You find a seat in the shadows and watch the busy activity of the inn. After a while, a tribesman wearing a white desert cloak sits down next to you. He looks at you and asks in a thickly accented voice if you are looking for a guide to take you to the Lost Quarter. You remain silent, and he leans closer towards you. 'Perhaps you are looking for the Lost Tomb of Kharphut the Mighty?' he whispers.

He offers you to lead you to the tomb for a fee of two gold pieces. If you have this amount and want to go with him, turn to **134**. If you haven't got the money, or would prefer not to go with him, turn to **10**.

The old man is right behind you as you go down the stairs. There is a light blue, corroded copper door in front of you, which he gestures to you to open. You do so, and find yourself in a large shrine room, with an altar in the centre and a door on the other side of the room. As you step into the room, you stand on a paving stone on the floor which suddenly depresses. There is a grinding noise, and you see stone slabs sliding down to block both of the doors. You may just have time to jump under the one nearest you.

You can either ignore the blocks and remain in the room (turn to **138**), throw down the urn and jump for the door (turn to **69**), or jump for the door, keeping hold of the urn (turn to **189**).

125

The jaguars are lithe, swift and lethal opponents. Unfortunately Gabbad is too old and infirm to help you in the fight. You must fight them one at a time.

JAGUAR   VIGOUR 9

Roll two dice:

score 2 to 3	Both jaguars manage to strike you; you lose 6 VIGOUR
score 4 to 7	One of the jaguars strikes you; you lose 3 VIGOUR
score 8 to 12	You strike the first jaguar; it loses 3 VIGOUR

Once you have defeated the first of them, turn to **23**.

126

The proprietor sticks out a brawny arm, stopping you dead in your tracks as you try to brush past him. He throws you back into the square and you land heavily; lose 2 VIGOUR. The owner dusts his hands off and goes back into the inn. If you are still alive, turn to **114**.

127

The dealer passes out the ivory chips used in the local gambling game. Excitement mounts as each player throws one of the chips on to the central table.

Roll two dice:

score 2	You are accused of cheating; turn to **187**
score 3 to 6	You lose your bet of two gold pieces; you must place another two gold pieces on the table if you wish to continue gambling (in which case roll again). Otherwise you must leave: turn to **48**
score 7 to 11	You win four gold pieces (twice your original stake). If you want to continue gambling place another two gold pieces as a bet and then roll again. If you want to leave, turn to **119**
score 12	You win the jackpot of ten gold pieces. If you want to continue gambling you must place another two gold pieces as a stake on the table, then roll again. If you want to leave, turn to **119**.

128

Getting over the wall with no equipment is easy. You drop down into a shadowy courtyard. A fountain can be heard splashing merrily at its centre.

Suddenly you sense movement in the shadows and you see a form sneaking up on you with a club raised high. Your assailant will surrender if you wound him *twice*.

SHADOWY ASSAILANT   VIGOUR 8

Roll two dice:
score 2 to 6   You are hit; lose 3 VIGOUR
score 7 to 12   Your opponent loses 3 VIGOUR

If you wound your opponent twice, turn to **191**.

129

Eventually you reach a point about halfway up the sand hill. To your surprise, you see in front of you a narrow, sand-choked stone entrance set into the side of it. The old man gestures for you to go into it. You light a torch and make your way down a steeply sloping sand shaft into the darkness.

You reach the bottom and find yourself in an ancient chamber, with hieroglyphics painted on the wall. The floor and most of one wall are covered with a great mound of sand that has been blown in by the desert winds. Looking up, you see that the old man is drifting down the mound of sand, without actually making any contact with it. He seems to glow eerily in the dark.

There is a set of steps leading down which are set into the floor of the room. The old man gestures you to precede him down it.

If you want to do so, turn to **124**.

If you would prefer to flee towards a door you can see in the left-hand wall of the room, turn to **137**.

130

You throw a gold coin into the stone offering bowl. The mouth of the stone sphinx opens and you hear it say: 'You have bought one question to which I will give the answer. Ask now, or forever hold your peace.'

There are a number of questions you could ask the sphinx:

If you would like to ask it about the Curse of the Pharaoh, turn to **205**.

If you ask which is the best route into the Lost Tomb, turn to **61**.

If you would like to ask about the best time to enter the Tomb, turn to **118**.

If you would like to ask it what equipment you will need to successfully accomplish your mission, turn to **34**.

131
You have just managed to relight your torch when you feel a sickening pain as something clawed rips open your back. Lose 6 VIGOUR. If you are still alive turn to **57**.

132
The corridor begins to spin round, and you begin to feel dizzy. You feel yourself being transported somewhere magically. Turn to **147**.

133
You hand over the gold pieces and the waiter goes off. You watch the antics of the belly-dancer. As she moves around the stage, members of the audience lean forward and hand her gold pieces. She is now opposite you. Do you, too, want to hand over a gold piece? If you do, turn to **143**, if you don't, turn to **217**.

134
The tribesmen pockets your two gold pieces and then gestures to you to follow him. You pass down dark alleyways; fierce dogs bark at you from the other side of locked doors and there is the smell of rotten garbage in the air. Soon you have left the busy bazaar area a long way behind you. The houses begin to thin out and you find yourself on the edge of the desert.

Without hesitation the tribesman steps off at a lively pace

across the sand. You walk for an hour and soon are lagging behind your guide. Just as you crest the top of a dune and look around for him in the barren moonlit landscape, you feel his hands grab your ankles and you are tripped up. You roll down the dune clutching at each other. You struggle free at the bottom of the slope, but you see that the tribesman has pulled out a knife. You can attempt to FLEE and turn to **37** after making your roll. Otherwise, you must face the tribesman in battle.

TRIBESMAN   VIGOUR 9

Roll two dice:
score 2 to 6   You are wounded; lose 3 VIGOUR
score 7 to 12   The tribesman loses 3 VIGOUR

If you win, turn to **112**.

135

You drink the potion (cross it off your Character Sheet) and drift one metre up into the air. You move forward, just over the top of the sculpted figures, and land in the clear space next to the door. Turn to **66**.

136

You feel half dead with horror as your Mirror Image slumps to the floor; but unlike you, he is totally dead. Searching the body you discover that your opponent had exactly the same equipment as you. You now have two of each of the items listed on your Character Sheet! You leave the room and ascend the staircase. Turn to **256**.

137

You may find it easier to run without the earthenware jar in your hands. If you want to drop the jar, turn to **41**. If you want to carry it with you, turn to **290**.

138

The slabs grind to a stop and you find yourself trapped with the old man in the shrine room. He turns towards you, his dark, hooded eyes boring into you. Suddenly you feel your hands begin to tremble and then the urn falls from them shattering on the floor into a thousand pieces. The old man gives a great hoot of evil laughter and then disappears. Looking down, you see what looks like a noxious gas issuing from the fragments. This gas forms itself into the shape of a malevolently grinning demon. It looks at you greedily. You have brought it here so that it can consume you in its own evil shrine room. You consider the irony of the situation as it moves into feast on you. Your adventure ends here.

139

Gabbad kneels beside the corpse and rolls back the man's cloak over his forearm. You see a coiled serpent tattooed on it. Gabbad looks up at you, his face creased with worry: 'It looks like the assassins are already after you: we must hurry to find the tomb before they do.' You set out for the desert and soon you are tiny dots moving over the huge, undulating surface of sand.

You travel for two days, eventually arriving at the end of a rocky gorge. You can see a pile of human bones in the middle of the pass. Your water is getting low and you will need to replenish it soon. You can see what looks like an oasis over to your left: a pool of blue surrounded by some date palms.

Do you want to go over to the oasis? Turn to **158**.

If you want to carry on through the pass, turn to **36**.

If you have one and would like to use it now, you can unroll your flying carpet here; turn to **4**.

140

After two more days in the desert, you pass through a narrow stony gorge and emerge in front of a small pyramid. There is a large sand-hill behind it. In the distance you can see an oasis and an avenue of stone sphinxes. The leader gestures you to enter a small stone building in front of the pyramid. Just as you step into its shadow, a hail of arrows descends on the party. You and the leader are protected by the overhang, but the two guards are killed instantly. You flee into the building. You are in a circular room. It is illuminated by a single beam of light descending from a small hole in a domed ceiling. At its centre is a plinth with a stone statue of an ancient pharaoh on it. A single gem has been set into the place where his eyes should be. There are stylised representations of the gods of Khem painted on the wall. A group of skeletons lie clustered around the plinth: they wear leather armour and still hold weapons clutched in their bony hands.

The leader of the assassins stands by the door fighting a white robed tribesman. You decide that this would be a good time to cut through your bonds, and you kneel on the floor sawing at the ropes with a sword held in one of the skeletons' hands. Eventually the rope parts. Just then the assassin's opponent falls to the ground, an object spilling from his hand and rolling towards you. You recognize the stone tablet! You quickly grab it up. The assassin swings round at you, threatening you with his sword, but you have already picked up one of the weapons lying on the floor. Just then, the sun descending from the hole in the ceiling strikes off the gem on the statue at the centre of the room, sending off a blinding light. You see a secret panel swing open in the wall and you dart towards it. The assassin leaps through it just as the stone slab swings back into place. For a moment you are left in complete darkness, and then you see a flash of tinder. Your adversary has lit a torch he was carrying. Seeing you, he lunges out with his sword. There is nowhere to FLEE to, so you must fight him.

ASSASSIN   VIGOUR 9

Roll two dice:
score 2 to 6   You are hit and lose 3 VIGOUR
score 7 to 12   The assassin loses 3 VIGOUR

If you win, turn to **9**.

141

You put the flute to your mouth and it plays, as if of its own accord, a hauntingly beautiful tune. You feel a sudden tug at the back of your tunic and you see the magical rope that you took from the tomb robbers snaking up to the ceiling from your backpack. Eventually it rests against the ceiling high above you. You pull at the rope; it seems quite rigid, as if it would take your weight. Do you want to climb up it? Turn to **271**. If you would prefer to walk back and explore the other branch of the corridor, turn to **238**.

142

You throw down the urn and turn to run. Unfortunately the urn shatters on a rock. What looks like a poisonous gas oozes out of it, resolving itself into the form of a malevolent demon. The jaguars stop in their tracks and crawl away whining; the old man vanishes into thin air with a shriek and you are left confronting a voracious demon against whom you have no power. Your adventure ends here.

143

You hold up your hand to her with the gold piece in it. She reaches out her bangle-covered arm and takes it. Just then, you feel a small object being slipped into your palm. Your hand clenches around it, you feel a small phial and you look at her in surprise. You see her stare at the phial and then nod her head at Leon's drink, next to yours on the table. Apparently she wants you to pour the contents of the phial into his cup.

Do you want to put the contents of the phial into Leon's

drink when he isn't looking? If you do, turn to **96**.

If you would prefer to carry on drinking with Leon, turn to **217**.

144

You momentarily lose consciousness as your body is thrown on to the hard, baked ground of the money has been stolen (cross it off your Character Sheet). You may try to go back to the inn, turn to **285**, or talk to the children playing in the square, turn to **190**.

145

You come face to face with two tomb robbers who have just walked around the corner of the corridor. They are naked except for turbans and loin-cloths. One of them is holding a rope which stands perpendicularly up into the air as if by magic. They are startled when they see you, but quickly raise their scimitars and rush in to attack you. You will have to fight them one at a time.

FIRST TOMB ROBBER   VIGOUR 8

Roll two dice:
score 2 to 6   You are hit and lose 3 VIGOUR
score 7 to 12   You hit the first tomb robber; because
                 he is not wearing any armour, he loses
                 4 VIGOUR.

If you defeat the first tomb robber, turn to **234**.

146

The beam of sunlight is no longer directly on the plinth, and the medallion no longer burns with a bright light. You can see that all the apples were in fact an illusion. There is a nest of writhing snakes on top of the plinth, surrounded by a layer of poisonous looking gas. If you would like to take the medallion, you may lift it up on the tip of your sword. Mark it down on your Character Sheet. You decide to leave the room and explore a corridor you can see leading away to the west. Turn to **84**.

147

You find yourself in a vast hall; stone rafters support a massive ceiling. A single ray of sunlight descends from some outlet hundreds of feet above you. At the far end of the hall you can see a ramp ascending a granite slope to a platform in the side of the wall. You can see an open entrance at the top of the ramp. There are two doorways on either side of the platform just before the sloping wall. The floor of the chamber has a number of small holes drilled into it. You prod the floor with your sword: suddenly there is a savage hissing sound, and a deadly dark asp, spitting venom, wriggles out of a hole and across the floor towards you. You crush it with your heel in revulsion. You realize that every time pressure is exerted on the floor near a hole, these asps will spring up.

To reach your goal you are going to have to cross the hall. You can either risk running across it, hoping that not too many asps will appear (if you do, turn to **177**), or you could use an item (turn to **21**).

148

You put the flute to your mouth and it starts to play a haunting tune of its own accord. The rope snakes up to the ceiling, where you can see the Pharaoh's ankh symbol etched on a stone. When you tug at the rope it feels stiff, as if you could climb up it. If you would like to do so, turn to **271**. If you would like to go back down the corridor and explore the other passageway, turn to **238**.

149

The carved stone skull over the lintel of the passageway fills you with dread. You start making your way down the corridor feeling for possible traps. Do you have a complete stone tablet with the Pharaoh's symbol on it? If you do, turn to **53**. If you don't, turn to **111**.

150

You feel the deadly poison of the asp spreading from the bite, but before it can reach your heart you suck the wound, spitting out the deadly venom. You have succeeded in pulling the lever, and you now turn and go up the steeply sloping corridor in front of you and enter a large audience chamber. Turn to **274**.

151

You elude the grasp of the outstretched hands. Looking back, you see that the old man is having some difficulties in following you. You see a ring set into one of the flagstones on the floor and next to it a rope. Pulling up the flagstone, you see a drop down to a passageway below you leading from the south to the north. Grabbing the rope and attaching it to the ring, you swing down into the darkness, landing safely in the corridor. You light a torch. Turn to **283**.

152

The snake sinks its fangs into your hand, but the glove protects it. You drop the snake on to the floor and it wriggles away into the darkness. Turn to **146**.

153

You drink the potion and rise slowly up into the air. You drift over the menacing holes to the far end of the hall. The effect of the potion wears off there, and you sink to the ground. Cross the item off your Character Sheet. Turn to **200**.

154

You come to a left-hand bend in the corridor. Your torch begins to gutter in a sudden breeze that is blowing down towards you. You feel that you must be very near the tomb chamber. Suddenly you see something huge sliding towards you down the corridor. It is a giant, blind worm, completely blocking the passage. You are just about to turn and run when a panel slides down with a thud behind you blocking your only means of escape. You are going to have to fight the worm.

GIANT WORM   VIGOUR 15

Roll two dice:

score 2   You are sucked into the creature's huge maw. A thousand bony teeth shred your flesh and your armour as you travel into its stomach. Your adventure ends here.

score 3 to 5   The creature begins to crush you against the wall. You can barely manoeuvre your weapon in the cramped confines. Turn to **78**, after first noting the worm's *current* VIGOUR.

score 6 to 12   You hit the creature: it loses 3 VIGOUR.

If you win, turn to **299**.

155

You wait, the stifling heat increasing in the close confines of the small room as it draws on to noon. The assassins look at you with increasing suspicion: they don't seem to believe you know how to enter the tomb. Suddenly there is a flash of blinding light as the beam of sunlight descending through the opening in the ceiling strikes off the gem on the statue. Your guards are blinded, but you notice a small slab swinging to one side in the wall near you. You slip through it, picking up a weapon from one of the skeletons as you do so. Unfortunately, the head assassin has seen you slipping away and leaps after you, just as the door closes with a dull thud behind you. After a moment of silence there is the dry scrape of tinder and a flame as he lights a torch. He rushes at you with his sword drawn when he sees you in the shadows. There is nowhere to FLEE, so you must fight him.

ASSASSIN   VIGOUR 9

Roll two dice:
score 2 to 6   You are hit and lose 3 VIGOUR
score 7 to 12   The assassin loses 3 VIGOUR

If you win, turn to **9**.

156
You thrust your hand into the mass of snakes, grabbing the lever. One of the snakes bites you on the wrist, and you lose 6 VIGOUR. If you are still alive, turn to **220**.

157
You just manage to roll under the door as the stone block comes grinding down with a thud, cutting you off from the old man. You walk back up the stairs to the room filled with sand and decide to investigate the door you saw earlier on. Behind the door is a room filled with old mummy cases. Finding a rope and a trapdoor set into the floor, you decide to explore the tomb a bit further. You attach the rope to a ring and let yourself down into a corridor you can see running along below you. You light a torch. Turn to **283**.

158
The oasis looks very tranquil, a gentle breeze plays over the date palms, their shade beckoning you from the desert sands. Gabbad mutters something about the Lost Quarter being full of magical sprites and monsters. You can see a single line of footprints leading to the edge of the water, but none returning. If you would like to carry on without any more

water, skirting the pass, turn to **164**. If you would like to go up to the oasis, turn to **97**.

159

You move around the edge of the room well away from the threatening-looking staff. You open the door to the next room. The floor of this room is covered with statues of servants and warriors one metre high. They're so closely packed together that it would be impossible to step through them without knocking one of them over. Something tells you this wouldn't be a good idea.

Do you have either a potion of levitation (turn to **216**) or a flying carpet (turn to **122**)?

If you have neither of those items, you will have to try jumping for a clear space that you can see in the centre of the room. It looks like you might then be able to jump from that space to another one by the door. If you do that, turn to **244**.

160

The tomb robber lies dead at your feet. The rope still hangs in the air. When you tug at it, it feels extremely firm, as if it would be possible to climb up the rope. The tomb robbers have apparently slain its owner somewhere ahead of you in the underworld. You remember one of them saying to his companion that the man who had had the rope had been playing a flute when they killed him. If you want to take the rope with you, mark it down as *a magical rope* on your Character Sheet. Now turn to **179**.

161

You stand on tiptoe and peer into the darkness beyond the hole, the only illumination being the light from the torch you are holding. In the glint of the torchlight you can see piles of furniture covered with gold-leaf, chariot wheels, ancient carved statues and a golden coffin. In the shadows there are two golden scorpions, and just below you in an open casket, you can see a beautiful gleaming stone in the shape of an eye. It sparkles magnificently in the light of the torch.

Do you want to crawl through into the room? If so, turn to **296**. If you would prefer to continue down the corridor to the west, turn to **193**.

162

A sudden chill seizes you as you run to the door. The ghost has cast a deathly curse on you. Roll two dice, trying to score equal to or less than your *current* PSI. If you succeed, turn to **261**. If you fail, turn to **278**.

163

You reach into your backpack and take out the flute, hoping to join in with the other players. However, your flute starts playing a different melody to theirs, and for a while there is a struggle of contrasting tunes until finally theirs fades away. Your flute also ceases to play and you are left in an eerily quiet chamber. You realize that you have just avoided being seduced by the spirits in it into abandoning your mission. You hurriedly leave by a doorway at the opposite side of the chamber. Turn to **90**.

164

You carry on through the burning heat, skirting around the rocky gorge. You drink some water, but still feel dehydrated. You lose 2 VIGOUR. If you survive, turn to **113**.

165

Do you have two halves of a stone tablet engraved with the Pharaoh's symbol? If so, turn to **221**. If not, you must step on to the dais, and turn to **245**.

166

You crawl back through the hole in the wall and turn to your right down the corridor leading to the west. Turn to **193**.

167

You can't believe that you will ever leave this place, so beautiful are the melodies that the ghostly flautists evoke. And indeed you won't for you have fallen foul of a magical spell that will keep you listening to the music until you die. Your adventure ends here.

168

You are going to have to run for it if you want to get away from him. It looks like you could hide in the small building in front of the pyramid below you. To help you run faster, do you want to drop the urn you are carrying? If so, turn to **276**. If you will run with the urn, turn to **104**.

169

You lift the medallion off the goblet with the tip of your sword. As its golden reflection ceases to play on the apples and the goblet, the apples turn into writhing snakes, and the goblet into a noxious, gas-filled container. You have nearly been tricked by a sorcerous illusion left here as a trap by the ancient magicians of long ago. You leave the room through the doorway to the west. A corridor stretches ahead of you. Turn to **84**.

170

You are cheered to see a light glowing from the entrance to the hut. Looking in, you see a woman with her back turned to you stirring some broth bubbling in a cauldron over a fire. She suddenly spins round, and to your horror you see that underneath her cowl her face is that of a spitting cobra and is not human at all! She holds a human liver in one of her hands. In the other she is clutching a hatchet. You are going to have to fight to the death: there is nowhere to FLEE to.

COBRA WOMAN   VIGOUR 6

Roll two dice:

score 2	She spits venom from her mouth on to your face. You fall to the floor paralysed and meet a ghastly end.
score 3 to 6	You are wounded by her hatchet; lose 3 VIGOUR
score 7 to 12	You hit her; she loses 3 VIGOUR

If you win the hut suddenly vanishes and you find yourself standing alone on top of one of the lonely dunes. There is no sign of the cobra woman or her hut. You have no option but to continue on your way. Turn to **39**.

171

You see the magical rope snaking its way upwards. It finally comes to rest leaning against the ceiling. You tug at it and it feels quite taut as if you could climb up it. If you would like to do so, turn to **271**. If you don't, turn to **287**.

172

Rather shaken from your encounter with the mummy you continue down the corridor and round the bend from where the tomb robbers appeared.

Turn to **179**.

173

Placing one of the items on the altar (cross it off your Character Sheet) you experience a sudden dizziness and the room starts to spin round. You are magically transported. Turn to **225**.

174

You climb the steps of the pyramid. The casket glows in your torchlight. You prise open the lid and find a curiously shaped key lying on a velvet cloth. Its handle is carved in a similar shape to that on your stone slab. You pick up the key. You can see no immediate use for it, but if you want to keep it, mark it down on your Character Sheet. You descend the pyramid and walk along the causeway to the arch in the west wall.

Turn to **249**.

175

The demon hurtles towards you, its supernatural shadows coiling around its scaly black flank. You are going to have to be very lucky to survive this encounter.

IPO: THE COILED SHADOWY HORROR
VIGOUR 24

Roll two dice:

score 2	The demon's darting tongue wraps around your face, blinding you. You quickly receive your death bite. Your adventure ends here.
score 3 to 7	You are bitten by the demon; you lose 4 VIGOUR
score 8 to 12	The demon loses 3 VIGOUR

If you win, turn to **93**.

176

You wait in the stifling heat; no sound breaks the utter silence of the desert. Suddenly there is a blinding flash of light as the sun strikes the gem set into the statue's forehead. Shielding your eyes from the intense glare, you see a panel slide up in the wall, and you step through it quickly. You find yourself in a granite vaulted chamber. A corridor leads off to the north into the darkness. You light a torch and set off up it. Turn to **283**.

177

You summon up your courage and sprint across the room. The asps fly out of their holes, and you feel their sharp teeth laced with deadly poison biting at your ankles as you run.

Roll two dice:

score 2 to 3   You are bitten several times by the snakes: the deadly poison courses through your veins and you collapse in their midst. You are powerless to resist their twisting bodies now as they feast on you. Your adventure ends here.

score 4 to 6   You are bitten a couple of times: deduct 6 VIGOUR

score 7 to 9   You are bitten once; deduct 3 VIGOUR

score 10 to 12   Miraculously, you avoid being bitten and reach the other side safely.

If you manage to get across to the other side of the hall, turn to **200**.

178

You realize that this is going to be a fight to the death anyway, so that your money won't be any good to you if you are the loser! You give the twenty gold pieces to some old man who is taking bets. He will give you two to one odds against you winning. If you win, you will not only get your twenty gold pieces back, but forty more as well. Setting your teeth into a grim smile you step into the swordsman's arena. Turn to **19**.

179

Turning left you see sunlight ahead of you. Eventually you come to a granite-walled room illuminated by a single shaft of sunlight coming from a hole in the ceiling high above you. The beam of light rests on a granite plinth. You see the sparkle of gold from the plinth and, moving closer, you see a golden goblet full of ruby-coloured wine, a number of golden apples and a sun-shaped medallion hanging from one of the handles of the goblet. Despite the colour of the apples, the food and drink seem extremely attractive to you as you are very thirsty and hungry by now.

Do you want to pick up the wine and an apple? Turn to **74**.

If you would prefer to lift up the medallion first, turn to **169**.

If you would rather continue down the corridor you can see through a doorway at the other side of the room, turn to **84**.

180

You start to fumble around the walls looking for a secret catch. Suddenly you press a secret panel and a spring is released, sending a hail of arrows thudding into your back, You black out, never to reawaken. Your adventure ends here.

You stare at the food unable to eat. Looking up, you find that the servants have vanished. You decide to leave this room, turn to **62**.

You wander for a length of time through the desolate moonlit dunes. Suddenly you hear a howling noise, and you see that there is a pack of hyenas streaming towards you over the dune. There is nowhere to FLEE to.

HYENA 1	VIGOUR 3
HYENA 2	VIGOUR 3
HYENA 3	VIGOUR 3
HYENA 4	VIGOUR 3
HYENA 5	VIGOUR 3
HYENA 6	VIGOUR 3

Roll two dice:

score 2	You are borne to the ground, and your throat is bitten open by one of the ravening animals; your adventure ends here
score 3 to 4	You receive a particularly unpleasant bite: lose 4 VIGOUR
score 5 to 6	You are bitten: lose 2 VIGOUR
score 7 to 12	You kill one of the hyenas

If you win, turn to **219**.

Gabbad shakes his head. 'You have broken into my house, and you have no money to pay me for the information that you require. This is shameful. The only way that this shame can be annulled and for you to pay me the money is if you go and face the Master Swordsman in the bazaar. If you beat him you will have enough money to buy my assistance.'

Knowing you have no option but to follow his suggestion, you allow yourself to be led back to the bazaar area by the little boy.

To your surprise, the bazaar square, which was virtually empty when you passed through it but half an hour ago, is crowded with black-cloaked figures, their features shadowed by their heavy cowls. They hold torches and seem to be heading for one particular spot where a large crowd has already congregated. The people stare at you and the boy curiously as you are the only ones not dressed like them. The boy ignores their stares and, taking you by the hand, leads you through the crowd to a bare circle at the centre of the mass of humanity. A grim looking swordsman, dressed from head to toe in black cotton material, stands with his arms crossed, a two-handed scimitar thrust into the ground next to him.

He eyes you critically through the eye pieces of his black mask. Seemingly reaching a decision, he throws you a bag. It lands at your feet with a chink. Picking it up, you find that it contains twenty gold pieces, exactly the amount you need. The swordsman will pay *you* to fight him: the crowd murmur expectantly as you hand the boy your cloak and draw your sword.

You see some of the crown exchanging bets. Do you want to lay a bet? If you do, turn to **178**. If you don't, turn to **38**.

184

You slip the gloved hand into the mass of snakes and grab the lever, yanking it up sharply. You then go up the steeply sloping corridor in front of you and enter a large audience chamber. Turn to **274**.

185

The feeling that you had of being able to see through the eye is lost when you drop it into the darkness of the backpack. Note that you have put it there and then move on to **166**.

186

With your last blow, the creature disintegrates into dust particles. You kick the mound of dust with your boot, but nothing stirs. You have an eerie premonition that the creature will return if you remain in the corridor for too long. There is a dark mirror at the end of the corridor; it gives off no reflection. When you reach out your hand to touch it, it passes right through the mirror.

Do you want to step through the mirror? If you do, turn to **281**. If you would prefer to return to the other corridor, and risk fighting the creature again, turn to **247**.

187

The one-eyed brigand spits on the table and jumps to his feet. 'Alright! I saw you slip that chip up your sleeve!' he yells at you as he pulls a rusty knife out of his belt and slashes at you with it.

THE DEALER   VIGOUR 9

Roll two dice:
score 2 to 6   You are hit and lose 3 VIGOUR
score 7 to 12   The dealer loses 3 VIGOUR

If you win, turn to **119**.

188

You take out the flying carpet and stand on it. You drift gently over the threatening holes in the floor of the hall, landing safely on the other side. To your disgust you notice that a thread of the carpet got snagged on the other side of the hall, and the carpet has almost totally unravelled. It is now useless, so cross this item off your Character Sheet. Now turn to **200**.

189

You dive towards the gap between the descending block and the floor. Roll two dice, trying to score equal to or less than your *current* AGILITY score. If you succeed, turn to **157**. If you fail, turn to **86**.

190

You approach the children, who stop running around as you draw near. They stare at you silently when you ask them if they know where the house of Gabbad, the dealer in antiquities, is. There is a silent pause and then one of the smallest children pushes to the front of the group. Although the other children are dressed in rags, this one is wearing quite a new cloak. He grins at you, whether in mischievousness or friendliness you cannot tell, and offers to take you to Gabbad.

If you would like to go with the boy, turn to **33**. On the other hand, you may reject his offer and go over to join the group of people by the fire-eater (turn to **214**), or go to the gambling den (turn to **218**), or to the inn (turn to **123**).

191

Your opponent drops his club and clutches his wounded arm. Just then his features are lit up as someone enters the courtyard carrying a lamp. The person you have been fighting in the darkness is dressed in a humble cloak and seems to be a servant. However, the old gentleman who has brought the light into the courtyard is obviously the master of the house. He peers at you through rheumy eyes. In the lighted doorway behind him you can see one of the small boys you noticed playing in the square earlier on. The old man asks you to explain yourself. You tell him as best as you can what your mission is and how you are trying to trace the stone tablet in your possession to its discoverer, Gabbad, collector of antiquities.

Although he seemed about to call out the city watch but a second ago, the old man hesitates when he hears his own name mentioned in connection with the stone tablet. He looks at you curiously. You suggest it would be a better idea to talk further on the subject indoors. He seems to resolve his doubts about you, and gestures you to follow him and the young boy into the house. The wounded servant follows you somewhat morosely. You suddenly remember your backpack on the other side of the wall. Gabbad opens the front door and you look for your equipment where you hid it, but it has vanished. You have now only your sword, a torch and the stone tablet. It seems that Leon got the better of you in the end. You seat yourself in a room with Gabbad and the young boy and explain your mission. Turn to **105**.

192

Eventually the corridor comes to a junction. There is a stone slab bearing the Pharaoh's symbol over the passageway in front of you. Next to it is a carved stone skull. You may either go straight on (turn to **149**), or turn to the right (turn to **29**).

193

A little further down the corridor, you see a section that has a number of deep recessed niches on either side of it. These niches contain statues representing the various gods of Khem. You recognize the jackal-headed god, and various other deities with animal features. The statues stand on low plinths with designs etched on to the face of them. There are two empty niches: stooping down you discover that one of them is devoted to the demon Bos, the bone cracker. To your surprise, you see that the design on front of the plinth shows the demon exchanging gifts with a man dressed in the tall hat, and holding the crook and mitre of the Pharaoh of Khem. The other plinth is dedicated to the demon Ipo, a snake deity represented by a coiled, shadowy serpent. It is wound round a man dressed in the same fashion as in the design on front of the Bos plinth.

If you would like to step on to the plinth dedicated to the demon Bos, turn to **58**.

If you would like to step on to the plinth dedicated to the demon Ipo, turn to **132**.

If you would prefer to continue down the passage to the west, turn to **209**.

194

The apparition beckons you over to it. It stares at you through its hollow eye sockets and addresses you in a chilling voice. 'Stranger, I will have your soul from you.'
It wants to gamble for your soul. Whoever gets the highest score on a single die roll will win it. Do you have the die with six sixes on it? If you do, turn to **260**. If you don't, turn to **108**.

195

The body of your opponent rolls down the steps to join that of his companion. You can see even in the gathering gloom that they both remain utterly motionless. You turn round and see the boy grinning at you, and you thank him for his help.

The houses on either side of you are eerily quiet now and you decide to press on as quickly as possible. The boy leads you to the top of the street and slips through the wooden door of an inconspicuous-looking house. You follow and find yourself in pitch darkness. The boy leaves you for a moment and you hear whispering from another room. Then you hear the sound of returning footsteps. Suddenly a light is struck and you find yourself staring into the tired old eyes of a white-haired man. Turn to **199**.

196

You down your potion, leaving Gabbad to be consumed by the jaguars. Unfortunately you soon become lost without him. A blinding sandstorm suddenly descends on you and you stumble around in it for a long time before you eventually succumb to exhaustion. Your adventure ends here.

197

There is a carved stone relief over the arch of the left-hand entrance. This depicts a skeletal figure gambling with a warrior. If you would like to continue under this archway, turn to **72**. If you would like to return to the right-hand archway, turn to **85**.

198

You pull out the golden medallion and hold it over the food. A golden aura spreads over the withered remains of the feast and to your amazement you suddenly see ruby red wine in the goblet, a freshly grilled chicken and various fresh fruits lying in baskets before you. Although you realize that this is just an illusion, you eat greedily; restore 6 VIGOUR but do not exceed your *normal* score. When you look up from eating, you find that all the servants have vanished. Turn to **62**.

199

'I am Gabbad,' he says. 'My nephew' - he indicates the boy - 'tells me that you want to find me. Well, here I am; speak your mind.'

You feel that you can trust him, so you pull out the stone fragment from the pocket of your tunic. Turn to **105**.

200

You start to ascend the ramp. Suddenly you hear a whistling noise that at first reminds you of the sound of wind blowing over the desert. The noise increases in intensity, becoming a high pitched whine. You look up to the top of the ramp: there, enveloped in a cloud of coiling shadow and driving sand, stands a huge serpent, rearing its head to the ceiling. Its darting tongue stretches two metres. You recognize it as Ipo, the Coiled Shadowy Horror. It starts slithering down the ramp towards you in intricate loops. This is going to be the toughest fight you have ever faced.

Do you have the magical staff? If you do, turn to **277**. If you don't, turn to **175**.

201

You find to your delight that you can now see behind you. Nothing is going to surprise you by sneaking up on you now. Make a note on your Character Sheet that you are wearing the magical eye on the back of your cloak and turn to **166**.

202

The heat of the desert is intense and you feel your strength ebbing away. Lose 3 VIGOUR points. If you are still alive, turn to **294**.

203

You are so hungry you would like to eat even the shrivelled remains of a feast set a thousand years ago. Unfortunately, you find the sight too repulsive and you leave the room still hungry.

Turn to **62**.

204

You make a tremendous leap and land in the clear patch. You are now standing at the centre of the room. You will have to leap again to reach the safety of the door. Roll two dice, trying to score equal or less than your *current* AGILITY rating. If you succeed, turn to **263**. If you fail, turn to **18**.

205

The sphinx tells you that you will need the other half of the stone tablet if you are to avoid the curse. The other half of the tablet is lost somewhere inside the tomb. If you would like to ask the sphinx another question, pay another gold coin and turn back to **130**. Otherwise, turn to **14**.

206

You resist being affected by the ancient magical spell in the staff. You can now pick it up safely. Make a note of it on your Character Sheet. You must also note that it has two *energy bolts* left to use. You hold up the staff and the next set of doors swings open automatically. You see a room filled with 1 metre high statues of servants and warriors. It doesn't look possible to step through the crowded figures to the door you can see on the far side of the room.

Do you want to clear a path through the room with an energy bolt from the staff? If you do, turn to **30**.

If you would prefer trying to jump across the room to where you can see a clear patch at its centre and then jump from there to another clear patch by the far door, turn to **101**.

If you want to lift up the staff and try to command the servants to do your wishes, turn to **226**.

207

You walk down the middle of the causeway between the two huge statues. Suddenly their arms swing together and it looks like that you will be crushed to pulp. Instead, the arms crash together and halt about six inches from your face. You duck under them and walk down the rest of the causeway, thankful for your narrow escape.

Do you now want to inspect the casket on top of the pyramid? If so, turn to **174**.

If you would prefer to skirt around the pyramid and walk over the other causeway to the arch in the west wall, turn to **249**.

208

You manage to stay ahead of the boulder. Suddenly it jams against the walls where the corridor narrows, completely blocking it. You cannot push the boulder aside.

You will have to go back to the platform and take either the right-hand archway, turn to **85**, or the left-hand archway, turn to **197**.

209

The passage is extremely long, but you eventually come to the head of a broad flight of steps leading downwards. The chamber in front of you seems vast and you start to descend the steps. Suddenly your torchlight catches the reflection of a large golden object in front of you, and the vast chamber is illuminated in a ghostly golden glow. The golden reflection is coming from a golden casket set on top of a small, stepped pyramid in the middle of a platform. The low platform is in the centre of a huge underground lake. A causeway leads across from the bottom of the steps to the platform. You can see another causeway leading to an arched entrance at the other side of the chamber. Two monolithic figures stand on the causeway between you and the platform. They are wooden statues, with stylised head-dresses and white tunics. They hold their arms slightly away from their bodies. It looks like someone might be either able to squeeze between them, or round to either side of them on the edge of the causeway. You can see curious pink logs floating in the water; when you look closer, you see these are actually albino crocodiles; they grin at you with snaggle-toothed mouths, eyeing you hungrily. There is a papyrus raft moored to your side of the underground lake, next to the causeway. A faint magical glow seems to pervade the air. You can:

Try to get round to one side of the statues blocking the causeway: turn to **60**.

Try to walk between the statues on the causeway: turn to **207**.

Try to punt the papyrus raft round to the platform, thus avoiding the statues but risking the crocodiles: turn to **214**.

210

You walk up to the huddle of country folk dressed in ragged nomadic cloaks who are watching the act in slack-jawed amazement. You stand amongst them and watch as the fire-eater touches a lighted brand to his lips and blow out a six foot gout of flame. Suddenly you feel a slight tug at the leather belt from which your purse hangs. You swing around to see a ruffian rushing off across the square waving your purse in his hand. Just as you're about to give chase, a man steps out of a doorway right in front of the thief, blocking his escape route. The thief falls over, dropping the purse, and scampers away into a back alley. You see the man pick up your purse and stroll over to you. As he comes closer you see he, like you, is wearing the short tunics fashionable to the North of this desert region. He introduces himself as Leon, a knight of your own country.

'Seeing that ruffian cut your purse, I knew I had to help a fellow countryman,' he explains. You thank him and he hands back the pilfered article. He offers to show you around the town but first of all insists on having a drink with you in the inn.

Do you want to go with him to the inn? Turn to **81**. If you don't, you could go up to the children playing in the corner of the square and ask their help (turn to **190**) or wait around until Leon has gone and then go into the inn (turn to **123**).

211

You drink some water and feel refreshed. Restore 3 VIGOUR points. You explore the other passageway; turn to **238**.

212

You are knocked backwards into the water by the wooden arm. You land right in the middle of the ring of snapping crocodiles. Your adventure ends here.

213

Taking care not to knock over any of the figures, you unfurl the carpet and step on to it. You drift over the figures to the door and open it. The carpet is now useless, so cross it off your Character Sheet. Turn to **66**.

214

You reach down and pull in the papyrus raft on its rope. The crocodiles appear to be ignoring you for the moment. You step into the boat and sit down in it, pushing off from the shore and paddling towards the central platform. Suddenly all the crocodiles in the pool seem to be swimming frantically towards you, their jaws outstretched. You are going to have to fight them off as best as you can. You concentrate your energy on one of them for the moment.

CROCODILE   VIGOUR 12

Roll two dice;

score 2 to 3   The crocodile upsets your raft and you fall into the water. You are soon torn apart by the creatures; and all that is left to remind other adventurers following in your footsteps of you is your cape floating on the surface of the water.

score 4 to 6   The crocodile bites you; you lose 3 VIGOUR

score 7 to 10   You hit the crocodile; it loses 3 VIGOUR

score 11 to 12   You manage to ram the paddle between the crocodile's jaws and it is immobilised; you have won.

If you beat one of the crocodiles, turn to **80**.

215

You just manage to dodge the massive, swinging wooden arm. The crocodiles snap disappointedly from where they are ringed around the spot where you would have landed if you had been knocked off the causeway. You walk down the remainder of the causeway, and on to the platform with the small, stepped pyramid.

Do you want to inspect the golden casket on top of the pyramid? Turn to **174**.

If you would like to skirt round the pyramid to the arched entrance at the end of the other causeway in the west wall, turn to **249**.

216

You drink the potion (cross it off your Character Sheet) and float up into the air until you are at a height just above the heads of the figures. You drift over them to the door at the far side of the room. You open the door and drift out into what must once have been a banqueting hall. There are shrivelled bits of meat on the plates on the table which must have sat there for hundreds of years. You come down to the ground as the potion wears off, and you decide to go further into the tomb.

Turn to **62**.

217

Leon continues to drink and chat with the people sitting at neighbouring tables. Eventually you are joined by a number of his friends: to your surprise you see him talking to the man who pickpocketed your purse earlier on. You are just about to get up and confront them both when you feel a sudden drowsiness overcoming you.

Roll two dice, and try to score equal to or less than your *current* PSI; if you succeed turn to **121**, if you fail, you black out (turn to **16**).

218

The men lounging by the door of the gambling den eye you critically as you walk up to the door, but they soon look away when your hand strays towards the hilt of your sword. You whip away the beads covering the door and stride down some steps into a smoke-filled room. You sit down at a table with some unshaven men. They are drinking heavily and seem to be argumentative. The dealer looks at you through his one eye, the other is covered by a patch, and says you must pay two gold pieces to join the game.

If you haven't got this money or don't want to pay it, turn to **48**. If you would still like to gamble, turn to **127**.

219

The dead animals lie scattered all around you. You sheathe your sword and set off grimly in the direction you believe the city to be in. Soon the dawn creeps up over the dunes and the day becomes bakingly hot. Do you have any water? If you don't, lose 3 VIGOUR points. At about noon you stumble back through the city gates. You collapse by a wall after drinking from a fountain and lapse into a deep sleep. You only wake up in the evening. You decide to go back to the bazaar. This time you are not going to trust any of the tribesmen to act as your guide. You decide to ask one of the children playing in the corner of the square where you might be able to find the house of Gabbad, the merchant of antiquities. Turn to **190**.

220

Roll two dice, trying to score equal to or less than your *current* VIGOUR score. If you succeed, turn to **150**. If you fail, turn to **95**.

221

You pull out the two halves of the stone slabs - the one showing the sceptre of the Pharaoh of Khem, the other his holy symbol, the ankh. You fit them together. Together they form a rectangular block that will exactly fit the gap at the foot of the coffin recess. If you want to put the two fragments together and place them in the niche, turn to **301**. If you would prefer not to, step on to the dais and turn to **245**.

222

You lift the sword and the sceptre from the glowing golden table: as you do so the ghost of the Pharaoh fades away, becoming invisible. Looking down at your gifts you see that they too vanish into thin air, leaving you with nothing. You wonder whether you made the wrong choice of the articles, but know that there is no way to find out. Your only course is to go further into the tomb, but do you want to take the right-hand or the left-hand exit from the chamber? If you want to go right, turn to **70**. If you want to go left, turn to **149**.

223

You take out the key. It seems to be attracted to the ceiling as if by a strong magnetic force. You can see the symbol of the Lost Pharaoh engraved on a stone slab set into the ceiling. If you have a magical rope and a flute, turn to **148**. If you don't, you must go to **238**.

224

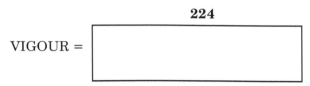

VIGOUR =

If you have just written a number in the box above, turn to **25**.

If there is already a number in the box, turn to **252**.

225

You find yourself in the middle of a room, the floor of which is covered with 1 metre high sculpted figures. The figures are of warriors and servants. You are hemmed in by them on all sides, and it would be impossible to step through them without knocking them over. There is a rectangular door made of burnished bronze with intricate patterns carved on it right in front of you. There is a small cleared area just in front of it. It looks like it might be possible to jump over to the clearing without disturbing any of the figures.

Do you want to risk jumping for the door? Turn to **254**.

You may prefer to use an item, on the other hand, in which case turn to **45**.

226

You lift the staff up before you. To your amazement, the figures of the servants and warriors suddenly spring up to life size people. They bow reverently to you and usher you through their midst, opening the set of doors on the other side of the room. You find the withered remains of some ancient feast laid out on the table here. The servants sit you down: one pours the dusty dregs of a pitcher of wine into your glass, whilst another one serves you the withered carcass of some age-blackened chicken. It will clearly be poisonous to eat or drink any of the material on the table.

Do you have the medallion shaped like the sun? If you do, turn to **198**. If you don't, turn to **181**.

227

You leap out of the alcove with a hoarse scream. One of the tomb robbers is so surprised that he doesn't react before you cut him down. His comrade, however, pulls out his sword and you are soon in a tense battle.

TOMB ROBBER   VIGOUR 12

Roll two dice:
score 2 to 6   The tomb robber strikes you; you
                 lose 3 VIGOUR
score 7 to 12   You hit the tomb robber; because he
                 is wearing no armour, he takes
                 4 VIGOUR points of damage.

If you win, turn to **160**.

228

You inhale a dose of the deadly fumes that waft out of the goblet in your hand. Lose 3 VIGOUR. You will feel dizzy for the rest of the adventure; deduct one point from your *current* AGILITY. If you are still alive, turn to **146**.

229

You reach the top of the sloping passageway and enter a large chamber. There are exits set into the right-hand and left-hand walls.

Turn to **274**.

230

Gabbad congratulates you on your victory and you walk down to the end of the rocky gorge with him. You continue for another mile or so. Ahead of you stretches an avenue of stone sphinxes. Behind the sphinxes there is a small pyramid, and behind that a large hill of sand reaches up to the desert sky. Gabbad tells you this is the place that he saw from the distance all those years before. You go over and inspect the avenue of sphinxes.

Turn to **56**.

231

You point the tip of the staff at the demon and fire one bolt of blue lightning energy at the creature, making its flank smoke with black noxious fumes. You have wounded it slightly, but it is still coming for you. (The staff is now useless, so cross it off your Character Sheet).

IPO: THE COILED SHADOWY HORROR
VIGOUR 18

Roll two dice:

score 2	The demon's darting tongue wraps around your face, its burning venom blinding you. Your adventure ends here.
score 3 to 7	The demon bites you; you lose 4 VIGOUR
score 8 to 12	The demon loses 3 VIGOUR

If you win, turn to **93**.

232

You wander for a few hours over the moonlit dunes. Eventually you see a lonely mud cottage standing all by itself on the dunes in the distance.

Do you want to approach it? If you do, turn to **170**. If you would prefer to ignore it, turn to **39**.

233

The sphinx tells you that you will need the other half of the stone tablet if you are to avoid the curse. The other half of the tablet is lost somewhere in the Pharaoh's tomb. If you would like to ask the sphinx another question, pay another gold coin and turn back to **280**, otherwise turn to **275**.

234

There is only one tomb robber left now, and he comes in to attack you.

TOMB ROBBER   VIGOUR 12

Roll two dice:
score 2 to 6   You are hit; lose 3 VIGOUR
score 7 to 12   The tomb robber loses 4 VIGOUR

If you win, turn to **160**.

235

You snuff out your torch and slide behind one of the decaying tapestries on the wall, almost choking on the cloud of dust you disturb. Peering through a hole in the tapestry you see two tomb robbers, walking down the corridor towards you. They are naked except for turbans and loin-cloths. They are jabbering away in an excited fashion to one another. Both of them are staring up at a rope that one of them is holding in his hands. The rope stands up perpendicularly and the person grasping it is having some difficulty in holding it down.

Do you want to leap out and make a surprise attack on them? Turn to **227**.

If you would prefer to let them pass down the corridor, turn to **268**.

236

Soon you reach the end of an avenue of sphinxes. Behind the avenue, you can see a small pyramid and behind that a small hill rising up towards the burning desert sky. You stop to inspect one particularly interesting sphinx, letting the old man continue to the end of the avenue ahead of you. It stands about two metres high and has strange hieroglyphic signs carved on its chest. There is an offering bowl between its paws and looking in you can see a number of gold coins lying at the bottom.

Do you want to reach in and pull out some of the gold coins? Turn to **32**.

If you have a gold piece and would like to throw it into the offering bowl, turn to **280**.

If you would prefer to ignore the sphinx and follow the old man to the end of the avenue, turn to **275**.

237

The only water you have left is the small amount in Ahmed's magical drinking bottle.

If you have got this, you drink from the bottle and restore 2 VIGOUR points, then turn to **116**.

If you haven't got the bottle, turn to **272**.

238

You walk down the dark corridor; your skin prickles at the nape of the neck as your feet disturbing centuries of dust. Suddenly there is a rush of ice cold wind and the dust swirls around you; your light goes put, leaving you in complete darkness. Cursing, you struggle to relight it, sweating despite the intense chill that has settled on the corridor.

Do you have a crystal eye attached to the back of your cloak? If you do, turn to **273**. If you don't, turn to **131**.

239

As you point the end of the staff at the statues of the servants, a blinding flash of blue lightning forks out of the end of it, vapourising them all. The staff has now got *two energy bolts* left. Note this down on your Character Sheet. You pass through the still smoking room to a banqueting chamber. An ancient feast was once laid out here, but all the food has withered into unappetising husks. Ignoring it you move on deeper into the tomb.

Turn to **62**.

240

You start your climb of the long ascending corridor. Suddenly your foot steps on a stone block on the floor which sinks down under your weight. Looking up, you see a huge boulder, as big as the corridor, rolling down towards you. You can see a gap in the wall, just to your right. Do you want to jump into it, hoping that the boulder will brush past you? If you do, turn to **43**. If you would like to run back down the corridor, turn to **89**.

241

You realize that you are now trapped. Something tells you to set the urn down on the altar in the centre of the room. You pull out the stopper blocking its top. A poisonous looking cloud of gas emanates from it. Gradually a demonic shape resolves out of the gas, and you see the form of the dreaded demon Bos the Bone Cracker rise up in front of you.

He yawns in a bored fashion. 'Time for the annual sacrifice again, is it?' he enquires. He casts malevolent purple eyes around the room. 'So, where's my sacrifice?' he says in an irritated fashion.

You realize that the sacrifice could be you, unless you

offer him something to placate him. Do you have the magical rope, the ornate flute, the key, or the crystal eye? If you have at least one of these items, turn to **248**. If you don't have any of them, turn to **289**.

242

The tomb chamber is a stunning sight. Its walls are covered in gold leaf; the glare from which, in your torchlight, is almost blinding. Mounds of jewels and ornaments lie stacked in lacquered boxes around the floor. Gorgeous circlets and crowns, kingly robes and gilt-framed mirrors increase the value of the haul. The treasure is surely worth not just a king's ransom, but the ransom of a whole dynasty of kings!

There is an alcove in the wall at the far end of the chamber. An even more brilliant radiance than that given out by the rest of the room emanates from here. Approaching closer, you see a golden coffin with a linen-wrapped mummy lying inside it. The walls of the recess are close to the side of the coffin, and there is a curious overhang at the level of the top of the coffin. Looking closely you can see many fragments of human bones littering the raised platform on which the coffin rests. Some of the bone fragments are now no more than powder having been, apparently, ground to dust. There is a high step up to the recess. In the front of the step is a space where a rectangular stone would fit. Over it are the symbols of the ankh and the Pharaoh's sceptre.

Do you want to step onto the dais and inspect the coffin? Turn to **245**.

If you'd prefer to get out an item first, turn to **165**.

243

Roll two dice, trying to score equal to or less than your *current* PSI. If you succeed, turn to **54**. If you fail, turn to **167**.

244

Your foot catches one of the servant statues, knocking it over. To your amazement the statue suddenly grows to a life-like size and you are confronted with a pale, mummified servant, his arms outstretched towards you, obviously intent on throttling you. You will have to defeat him before you can get to the other side of the room.

MUMMIFIED SERVANT   VIGOUR 9

Roll two dice:
score 2 to 6   The servant hits you, you lose 3 VIGOUR
score 7 to 12   The servant loses 3 VIGOUR

If you win, turn to **246**.

245

There is a sudden click as you step on to the platform. The walls suddenly snap together, like protective jaws over the mouth of the coffin. You, unfortunately, are standing in the way of these stony jaws and you are crushed into a jelly. Once more the curse of the Pharaoh, that strikes down all the unwary and over-greedy, has accounted for an intruder into the impregnable tomb. Your adventure ends here.

246

The servant falls backwards with a hollow groan. You must now make another leap to reach the door. Roll two dice, trying to score equal to or less than your *current* AGILITY. If you succeed turn to **263**. If you fail turn to **18**.

247

You pass the junction where you joined this passageway, and find the corpse you saw before lying at the end of the corridor. Do you have an ornate flute? If you do, turn to **73**. If you don't, turn to **94**.

248

You proffer one of the items (cross it off your Character Sheet) placing it on the altar in front of the demon. This seems to satisfy him. He waves his purple fist in front of you and you feel the room beginning to spin round. Turn to **225**.

249

You walk underneath the huge brick archway and down a short length of corridor. The corridor soon joins another passage that runs across it at right angles. You peer down it in both directions. It is a brick-lined passageway, similar to the one you have just walked down. You can just about make out the form of someone lying on the floor a few yards down the corridor to your left. Nothing is visible down the corridor to your right. You must turn right or left as the passage that you are in does not continue in front of you.

If you want to go right, turn to **238**.

If you want to go left, turn to **257**.

250

You just manage to pull your hand away in time. Deciding that you have had enough of the sphinx, you walk down to the end of the avenue. Turn to **31**.

251

You drop the snake and the goblet just in time; the gas dissipates with a murderous hiss and the snake writhes away over the floor. Shaken by your narrow escape, you decide to look at the plinth again. Turn to **146**.

252

You enter a dimly lit hall: magical lighting throws huge shadows of yourself against the walls. Your own torch dims. From the darkness at the end of the hall you see a warrior dressed in a soiled white desert cloak, his armour caked with white dust striding towards you. You suddenly realize that the warrior is a mirror image of yourself! You must fight him.

MIRROR WARRIOR   VIGOUR __ *

*For the VIGOUR of the Mirror Warrior, refer to **224** and write the score that is in the box there into the space above.

Roll two dice:

score 2 to 6   Your Mirror Image strikes you, you lose 3 VIGOUR

score 7 to 12   The Mirror Image loses 3 VIGOUR

If you win, turn to **136**.

253

Seeing his companion dead on the floor, your other assailant runs past you and dashes out into the square. You follow, and catch a glimpse of him disappearing down an alleyway. Deciding that he is not worth pursuing, you go over to talk to some children playing in a corner of the square. Turn to **190**.

254

Roll two dice, trying to score equal to or less than your *current* AGILITY. If you succeed, turn to **263**. If you fail, turn to **18**.

255

You place a variety of objects on the altar, but nothing happens with any of them. You try to kick through the doors, but they are made of solid bronze. After a few days you die of hunger. Your adventure ends here.

256

You reach the top of the staircase, sweating heavily from exertion. The temperature seems to have risen, and you realize you must be inside the pyramid of Kharphut the Mighty, and quite near the surface. The stairs double back on themselves and go up to another landing and then double back on themselves again.

Looking over the balcony of one of the flights you realize that the entrance hallway must be hundreds of feet below you. Eventually you reach a set of large bronze double doors. You notice with horror that the bronze is emblazoned with the sacred glyphs and runes of the demon Bos. Taking your courage in your hands, you step through the doors. They shut with a flat metallic clang behind you. You are in a large room, with reliefs of the foul demon Bos carved all over the walls. There is another set of doors in front of you. There is a large altar in the centre of the room.

Did you once have an urn that an old man asked you to carry for him in the desert, but no longer have it? Turn to **27**.

If you still have the urn, turn to **241**.

If you have never had an urn, turn to **292**.

257

Turning to the left, you walk up to the prostrate figure that you saw from the junction. The corridor finishes in a dead end just beyond the figure. There is a rough rock face, with baskets full of rubble, picks and adzes littered around as if the workmen had only recently abandoned their attempts to lengthen the tunnel. The figure is dressed in dusty robes. A number of rather jagged knives protrude from his blood-soaked back. One of his arms is outstretched. Next to it you can see an ornate ivory flute. It seems to have broken in two halves when the man fell. However, when you pick it up (note it on your Character Sheet) you can see that the flute is so designed that it is possible to screw the two halves back together again.

Do you want to screw the flute back together again and try playing it? If you do turn to **73**.

If you would rather go back and explore the other branch of the corridor, turn to **238**.

258

Do you have the snake-proof gloves? If you do, turn to **184**. If you don't, turn to **156**.

259

Your sword passes right through your opponent's black cloak and he topples over. Instead of a cheer of approval from the crowd, however, your victory is greeted with a deadly silence. The small boy runs up to you and, taking you by the hand, leads you through a gap in the crowd that opens as if by magic in front of you. You pass through a sea of staring faces. No one moves to follow you as you break through the outer ring of people and are guided down the back alleys. Soon you are back at Gabbad's house. Turn to **59**.

260

The apparition rolls its dice, rubbing its bony hands together in anticipation. It scores a four and chuckles gleefully. You throw your dice which, naturally, scores a six. The ghost disappears with a moan of disappointment.

Turn to **261**.

261

You rush out of the room, your heart beating wildly. You are thankful to have survived. You find a corridor that leads upwards and follow it.

Turn to **192**.

262

You insert the key in the lock and it turns easily. The door swings open to reveal a wooden panelled chamber. A staff, shaped like a pharaoh's crook hovers in mid-air in front of you. It is surrounded by an aura of shimmering blue light. You advance into the room and the light dies down. You seize the staff and you feel the power of ancient magic thrumming through your fingers. Mark it down on your Character Sheet and note that it is charged with 3 bolts of energy. The double doors in front of you swing open revealing a room filled with one-metre-high wooden figures representing warriors and servants. They are all bowing towards the door in which you are standing. You feel that the staff that you are holding will somehow clear a path through the figures if you aim it at them.

If you would like to try this method of getting through the room without touching the figures, turn to **239**.

If you would like to hold up the staff and try to command the figures to follow your orders, turn to **226**.

263

You just manage to make it to the clear patch by the door. You swing the heavy door open, and pass through a banqueting hall, turn to **62**.

264

One of the scorpions lashes its tail into your exposed hand before you have time to withdraw it. You feel poison coursing up your veins. You lose 6 VIGOUR points. If you are still alive, you decide that you have had enough of the sphinx. You walk down to the end of the avenue. Turn to **31**.

265

You pull out the medallion. Perhaps if it created illusions of food before, it will help you eat the food on the table. Sure enough, the minute you place it on the table the dust-choked goblets seem to fill with wine, the blackened carcasses on plates become freshly grilled chickens, and the shrivelled husks in the fruit bowls become grapes, apples and freshly

picked oranges. You eat and drink your fill. Restore 6
VIGOUR points (but do not exceed your *normal* score). After
you have eaten, turn to **62**.

266

If you have them, you may take out either the key (turn to
223) or a magic water bottle (turn to **211**). If you don't have
either, you decide to explore the other end of the corridor,
turn to **238**.

267

You eventually manage to break the door down with your
sword. Sweating from the exertion, you step through the
hole in the splintered wood. You have entered a panelled
room. Another door, unlocked this time, stands before you.
Hovering in the middle of the room and surrounded by an
aura of blue light, you see a staff shaped like a pharaoh's
crook.

Do you want to try to pick up the staff? Turn to **52**.

If you would prefer to skirt around it and go the door,
turn to **159**.

268

You let the tomb robbers pass by the alcove. You hear them
discussing how they killed the owner of the magical rope
somewhere ahead of you in the underworld. Their voices
recede into the distance and you are just about to step back
into the corridor when you feel a bandage-swathed arm
clamp on to your shoulder. You swing round to find yourself
confronted with a bandage-clad mummy staring at you
through a slit in the cloth wound round his head. He holds a
wickedly curved dagger in one of his hands. You must fight
him.

MUMMY   VIGOUR 12

Roll two dice:

score 2 to 6   The mummy strikes you; you lose 3 VIGOUR

score 7 to 12   The mummy loses 3 VIGOUR

If you win, turn to **172**.

269

The warrior topples over, transformed back into a statue. It crashes into the other figures who all begin to squirm into life. You realize that you are going to have to vacate the room in a hurry. You run to the door.

Turn to **66**.

270

You take the sword and the stone from the glowing, golden table. As you do so, the Pharaoh fades from view. Looking down, you see that the sword has also disappeared, leaving you with only the other half of the stone tablet. You press the ragged edge of this to the broken edge of the tablet you already have and find that they fit together perfectly.

You can now leave by either the left-hand door, turn to **149**, or the right-hand door, turn to **70**.

271

The rope remains firm when you climb up it. You find a stone slab marked with the Pharaoh's symbol on the ceiling. This swings back when you push it up and you find yourself in a small stone chamber. There is an ornately carved doorway in front of you, framed by reliefs of two eagles with their wings outstretched over the lintel. There is a large keyhole on one side of the door.

Do you have the key with a handle carved in the shape of the Pharaoh's symbol? If you do, turn to **262**. If you don't turn to **267**.

You are now extremely thirsty. You lose 3 VIGOUR; if you are still alive, turn to **116**.

The eye brings into focus a large leonine form caked in white dust, with taloned claws, a flowing mane, but with a half human face and a fur covered human body approaching you from behind. It holds an evilly curved knife in one of its paws. The knife glints in the light of your recently rekindled torch. In its other paw it carries a fresh human heart. You swing round and find that the reality of the creature is, if anything, more frightening than the image of it in the crystal eye. You must fight it.

THE EATER OF HEARTS   VIGOUR 15

Roll two dice:

score 2	The creature stretches out one of its clawed paws, ripping the living heart from your body. You are killed instantly.
score 3 to 6	You are wounded by the creature's knife; lose 3 VIGOUR
score 7 to 12	The Eater of Hearts loses 3 VIGOUR

If you win, turn to **186**.

There is a throne set against the wall to the north of the chamber. An old man with a withered face, wearing the mitre hat of the Pharaoh of Khem sits on it under a huge, stylised sun ornament set into the wall. The Pharaoh gestures at you to approach him and you do so. He looks at you for a moment, then opens his bloodless lips.

'Many men have tried to enter my tomb. Only a few have reached this room,' he says. 'As a consequence, I will grant you two gifts, for you have shown courage in getting so far.'

He points to the floor and a golden table appears, laden with costly goods. On it you can see a gleaming sword, a sceptre shaped like a blazing golden sun and the missing half of the stone tablet that you brought with you from your homeland in the north. Carved on the stone is a sceptre, similar to the one lying on the table. Which of the items will you take?

If you want to take the sword and sceptre, turn to **222**.

If you want to take the sword and the stone, turn to **270**.

If you want to take the sceptre and the stone, turn to **79**.

275

The old man has been waiting for you at the end of the avenue of sphinxes. You can see a low building to your left in front of a small pyramid. It is nearly midday and the sun is very hot. The old man leads you up the side of the small hill behind the pyramid.

Do you want to go any further with him? If you do, turn to **129**. If you don't, turn to **168**.

276

You throw down the urn and it shatters on a rock standing up from the sand. You can see a cloud of what looks like purple poison gas oozing out of the shattered bits of pottery. The gas resolves itself into the shape of a savage demon. The old man shrieks and disappears into thin air. The demon hovers over you, ready to rend you limb from limb. Your adventure ends here.

277

How many energy bolts has the staff got left?

Three?	Turn to **100**
Two?	Turn to **8**
One?	Turn to **231**

278

A deadly chill freezes your blood and you black out. Your adventure ends here.

279

To your amazement, you hear voices coming from behind a bend in the corridor in front of you. Whoever is speaking are coming towards you. Do you want to extinguish your light and hide in one of the alcoves? If so, turn to **235**. Or will you advance boldly down the corridor? If so, turn to **145**.

280

You throw a gold coin into the stone offering bowl. The mouth of the stone sphinx moves and you hear it say, 'You have bought one question to which I will give you the answer. Ask now, or forever hold your peace.'

There are a number of questions you can ask the sphinx:

If you would like to ask if about the old man you are with, turn to **7**.

If you would like to ask it about the Curse of the Pharaoh, turn to **233**.

If you would like to ask about the best route into the Lost Tomb, turn to **91**.

If you would like to ask about the best time to enter the Tomb, turn to **6**.

If you would like to ask it what equipment you will need to successfully accomplish your mission, turn to **92**.

281

Turn to **224**. There is a box marked 'VIGOUR' there. Write down your *current* VIGOUR score in it.

282

The next day the guards return. They drape a heavy white nomad cloak over you, keeping your hands tied behind you. You feel the sharp points of swords pressed against your back as you pass through the narrow streets of the city: to call out would lead to instant death. What is more, the heat of the sun in the desert is soul-destroying and your captors don't give you any water.

Lose 3 VIGOUR. If you survive, turn to **99**.

283

You pass down the corridor, grateful for the light shed by your torch. The air in the underground passageway is close and musty, as if it hadn't been disturbed for a thousand years. Eventually you realize that the corridor must be leading you right under the hill at the back of the large pyramid. The hill is, in fact, a gigantic pyramid, that of the Lost Pharaoh, Kharphut the Mighty! The corridor begins to sport crumbling tapestries on its walls. Soon you can make out dusty alcoves filled with crumbling armour and junk behind the tapestries.

Turn to **279**.

284

The two jaguars are lithe and subtle opponents; they fight with wicked claws and sharp fangs. You must fight them one at a time.

FIRST JAGUAR   VIGOUR 9

Roll two dice:

score 2 to 3	Both jaguars manage to strike you; you lose 6 VIGOUR
score 4 to 7	One of the jaguars strikes you: you lose 3 VIGOUR
score 8 to 12	You strike the first jaguar; it loses 3 VIGOUR

Once you have defeated the first one, turn to **11**.

285

You are stopped at the door of the inn by the proprietor, a large brawny man who obviously doesn't want any trouble from the likes of you.

Do you want to try to re-enter the inn? Turn to **126**.

If you would prefer to wander over the square to where the group of children are playing, turn to **190**.

286

The flute plays a beautiful, haunting tune evoking long distant times. Nothing else happens. Turn to **266**.

287

You look back down the corridor; the monster that attacked you has not yet reappeared. You rush back to the mirror at the end of the other passageway and pass through it. Turn to **281**.

288

You find yourself not in the alcove any more, but in a large chamber, with etched reliefs along its walls and an altar in the centre. There are two sets of locked doors at either end of the room; you are trapped.

If you once had an urn that an old man asked you to carry for him, but no longer have it, turn to **27**.

If you still have the urn, turn to **241**.

If you have never had the urn, turn to **292**.

289

The demon decides to take the annual sacrifice by devouring you! Your adventure ends here.

290

You rush towards a door, barging it with your shoulder. You burst through the rotten boards, fragments of wood spraying out to either side of you. You find yourself in a narrow room choked with thick tendrils of dusty cobwebs; a number of mummies lie swathed in linen bandages in coffins arranged to either side. The room is effectively a corridor leading to another door. You rush down the central aisle, but suddenly you feel bandage-swathed fingers reaching out and grasping your tunic. At the same time, you are entwined in the thick cobwebs. You are going to have to be very agile to elude the twin grasp of both the mummies and the cobwebs.

Roll two dice, trying to score equal to or less than your *current* AGILITY. If you succeed turn to **151**. If you fail, turn to **13**.

291

The only difference in having the eye on the front of your cloak is that now you see things in triplicate!

If you would like to fasten it on to the back of your cloak instead, turn to **201**.

If you would like to drop it into your backpack, turn to **185**.

If you would like to leave it where it is, turn to **166**.

292

You decide that you will never escape from this room unless you make some kind of sacrifice on the altar. Do you have any of the following items: a magical rope, an ornate flute, a crystal eye or a key? If you do, turn to **173**. If you don't, turn to **255**.

293

You both drink the potions and start to run. You easily outstrip the jaguars, and are pleased to see Gabbad still at your side. You run for a couple of miles and eventually find yourself at the end of a long avenue of sphinxes. You can see a small pyramid in the distance, with a larger hill standing behind it. You pass down the avenue and see a small building in front of the first pyramid. Suddenly Gabbad stumbles against you and falls to the ground. The heat has taken its toll on the old man and he has died of exhaustion. Sadly you bury him, but know you must continue with your task before you meet the same fate. You enter the building through a low door. Turn to **35**.

294

The heat doesn't seem to bother the old man at all and he continues at his unflagging pace. Soon you come to a narrow gorge through some rocks. The gorge is littered with human bones. Unperturbed, the old man starts off down it with you following, clutching the urn. Suddenly there is a blur of movement to one side of you, and you see two jaguars racing towards you over the rocks. They seem to be ignoring the old man completely, so you will have to fight *both* of them if you stand and face them.

Do you want to run, carrying the urn with you? Turn to **109**.

Or would you prefer to drop the urn and run? Turn to **142**.

If you would prefer to fight the jaguars, turn to **284**.

295

The bolt of blue coruscating flame envelopes you, searing your flesh. You black out with the pain. Your adventure ends here.

You wriggle through the narrow gap and drop down into the musty room. You manage to avoid tripping over the piles of junk at your feet and reach out your hand to pick up the beautiful, gleaming eye in the casket. Suddenly you hear a strange metallic clacking sound. Looking up you see that one of the scorpions has come to life, its pincers extended towards you. You cannot flee this combat.

MECHANICAL SCORPION   VIGOUR 12

Roll two dice:

score 2	The tail of the scorpion whips up from behind it, stabbing you in the chest. Some vicious poison concocted thousands of years ago by the ancients, courses through your veins. You die in seconds.
score 3 to 6	One of the scorpion's mechanical pincers clamps on to one of your limbs. The pincers are razor sharp; you lose 3 VIGOUR
score 7 to 11	You hit the mechanical scorpion; because of its metallic skin, it only loses 2 VIGOUR
score 12	You hit some sensitive spot of the creature's mechanism and it stops dead.

If you win, turn to **71**.

The next morning you are woken early by the old man. He is dressed in a desert cloak and has a water flagon strapped to his belt. He hands you a similar cloak and flagon. Note these down on your Character Sheet. The water may be especially important to you in the desert. The merchant hands over the keys to his shop to his young nephew and you step outside. A washerwoman is coming towards you down the narrow alley, otherwise it is deserted. Suddenly the 'washerwoman' whips out a dagger and you see that she is actually a man in disguise. You barely have time to lift your sword in defence before the assassin is upon you. You cannot FLEE.

ASSASSIN   VIGOUR 9

Roll two dice:
score 2 to 5   You are hit; lose 3 VIGOUR
score 6 to 12   The assassin loses 3 VIGOUR

If you win, turn to **139**.

298
All through the night and the morning of the next day, the old man glides in front of you, his feet hardly seeming to touch the ground.

It is getting very hot. Have you got any water? If you have, turn to **2**. If you haven't, turn to **202**.

299
You climb over what remains of the worm and continue down the corridor to the left. Soon you come to a magnificent set of double doors covered with gold leaf. You can see your own reflection in it in the light from your torch. Instinctively you know you have at last arrived at the tomb chamber of Kharphut the Mighty, the Lost Pharaoh. The doors swing open at your touch. Turn to **242**.

300
Your opponent clutches his wounded arm and begs you for mercy. You suddenly see a light being carried across the yard towards you. It is held by an old man who peers at you with rheumy eyes. You see a small boy standing staring at you

from a lighted doorway into the main part of the house. The old man asks you to explain yourself. You tell him as best you can about your mission and how you are looking for Gabbad, the merchant of antiquities. You pull out the stone tablet and hold it out to him; he seems to start with surprise when his eyes eventually focus on it.

'I thought never to have seen that stone again,' he says in a hushed voice, 'If you want my help then you will have to pay for it; I have already suffered enough through that stone to be wary of meddling with it again.'

He mentions a fee of twenty gold pieces. Do you have this amount? If you do turn to **59**. If you don't, turn to **183**.

301

You place the two halves of the tablet into the alcove. There is the noise of stone blocks falling away, and a blaze of light as the sun bursts through an opening that has appeared above the coffin almost blinds you. You see that the body of the Pharaoh is dissolving into a white mist as the light burns into it. The mist wreaths upward and out into the desert air. The Pharaoh's spirit has been liberated and will now drift across the sands. A beautiful jewelled sceptre lies in the coffin where his head was. You pick it up and turn back to the darkness to see if you can get hold of any more treasure.

Suddenly there is tremendous rumbling noise, and great blocks of masonry begin to fall into the room, crashing on top of the caskets and the mounds of gems. Clearly you are not going to have time to recover any more of the fantastic wealth of the tomb if you wish to survive. You quickly climb on top of the coffin and lever yourself out of the opening above you. You find yourself on top of the large hill that stood behind the smaller pyramid in the desert. You realize now that the hill was actually the vast pyramid tomb of the Lost Pharaoh. Suddenly the top of the sand hill begins to cave in on itself as the ancient blocks collapse beneath you. You race down the side of the dune, the masonry collapsing just a second behind you. You lose your footing and roll to the bottom, stopping abruptly as you bump into someone's legs. Looking up and squinting your eyes into the blinding desert sunlight, you see one of the grim-faced desert nomads standing over you, a vicious curved sword in one of his hands.

Looking around, you see that you are surrounded by the tribesmen. Suddenly, remembering the sceptre, you hold it up before their eyes. With a gasp they step back and to your surprise they bow low in front of you, throwing their weapons at their feet. Within minutes, you are on a camel, and the tribesmen are leading you in triumph back to the city of Arkos. Looking back, you see a cloud of sand hanging in the air as the pyramid continues to collapse in on itself, burying forever the Pharaoh's guardians, and the curse that cost so many warriors their lives.

THE END

FABLED LANDS

A sweeping fantasy role-playing campaign in gamebook form

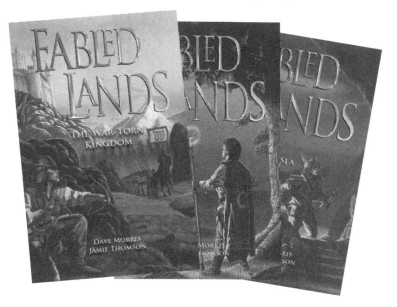

Set out on a journey of unlimited adventure!

FABLED LANDS is an epic interactive gamebook series with the scope of a massively multiplayer game world. You can choose to be an explorer, merchant, priest, scholar or soldier of fortune. You can buy a ship or a townhouse, join a temple, undertake desperate adventures in the wilderness or embroil yourself in court intrigues and the sudden violence of city backstreets. You can undertake missions that will earn you allies and enemies, or you can remain a free agent. With thousands of numbered sections to explore, the choices are all yours.

Made in the USA
Columbia, SC
27 February 2021